JOURNEY INTO LOVE

Steve Westwood, who ran an investigative agency with his friend Mike, was asked by a solicitor to trace a Lexie Bennett as she had been left a considerable fortune. After following several leads, Steve eventually found Lexie working in a pub in a border village in Scotland. But she made it quite clear that she did not want to be found. Why would a beautiful girl like her want to hide herself away? Steve was determined to discover the reason . . .

Books by Margaret McDonagh
in the Linford Romance Library:

MARGARET McDONAGH

◆

JOURNEY INTO LOVE

Complete and Unabridged

LINFORD
Leicester

First published in Great Britain in 1997

First Linford Edition
published 1998

British Library CIP Data

McDonagh, Margaret
    Journey into love.—Large print ed.—
    Linford romance library
    1. Love stories
    2. Large type books
    I. Title
    823.9′14 [F]

    ISBN 0–7089–5404–9

Published by
F. A. Thorpe (Publishing) Ltd.
Anstey, Leicestershire
Set by Words & Graphics Ltd.
Anstey, Leicestershire
Printed and bound in Great Britain by
T. J. International Ltd., Padstow, Cornwall

This book is printed on acid-free paper

For Pam and Alan, with love

For Paul and Alan, with love

1

Steve Westwood glowered at the clock on the wall of the plush reception area. He did not appreciate being made to wait, as if his time was less valuable than that of the man he was here to see.

If his partner, Mike Adams, hadn't twisted his knee protecting a VIP at a political rally turned hostile, it would not have been necessary for him to alter his own plans and keep this appointment in Mike's place.

As it was, the half hour he had already been sitting here could have been put to better use following up work he had in hand or tackling the mountain of paperwork on his desk that increased in volume with each passing day.

His ash-grey gaze swept round the waiting area, taking in the marbled floor, the original, abstract paintings that adorned the professionally-decorated walls, the expensive, environmentally-unsound hardwood furnishings. Everything spelled wealth — wealth and power.

The blonde secretary who sat behind a vast desk equipped with computer, Fax machine and switchboard, cast a speculative glance at him, open interest in the heavily-mascaraed eyes.

Steve returned the stare, his own discouraging and impassive. The woman did not appeal to him.

His temper simmering, he looked pointedly at the clock once more. The secretary chewed her thin, scarlet lips, clearly at a loss as to whether to remind her boss yet again of Steve's arrival.

Steve knew little about the man he was waiting to see. The brief Mike had given him had been sketchy at best, and there had been no details forthcoming on the reasons for the summons to these posh London offices. The legal firm was not familiar to him and was not one they had worked for in the past.

He and Mike had met when they had joined the army and had been friends ever since. They made a good team, their differences complementing each other rather than causing friction.

Already disenchanted with the life, Steve had left the army when Mike, married with a young family, had decided to embrace civilian domesticity and put down more permanent roots.

Together they had set up in business. It had been hard at first, but was now proving to be the best decision they had ever made. They had not anticipated involving themselves in anything other than security, protection and consultancy work, but a one-off request to help trace a missing person had been successful and had given birth to a useful, investigative sideline. So much so, they had taken on extra staff at their agency.

After their rocky start, their professionalism, integrity and success had given them a good name and thanks to word of mouth and recommendations, they now had an impressive client list. Impressive and growing. Things were looking good for the future.

'Mr Westwood?'

Steve directed his attention away from his thoughts and watched as the secretary rose to her feet, smoothing down the hem of her hip-hugging skirt.

'Mr Apostolakis will see you now.'

He followed her to an ornate pair of doors. She swung them inwards with practised ostentation and gestured him to enter. Steve found himself in a room which was approximately the size of their entire agency suite. It was thickly carpeted and even more expensively appointed than the waiting area he had just vacated.

His gaze settled on the man who stood up from the chair behind the leather-topped desk at the far end of the office.

Short and squat, the middle-aged Greek had a thatch of dark hair and a neat beard and moustache. The partially obscured mouth curved in brief acknowledgement of Steve's presence but the dark brown eyes beneath coarse, bushy eyebrows were cold and remote.

'I am sorry to have kept you,' the man said, his voice high-pitched and with only a faint trace of an accent.

Steve accepted the offered handshake but made no response to the insincere platitude.

'How can we be of service to you?' he asked, seating himself in the chair nearest him and coming straight to the point.

'A delicate matter, Mr Westwood.'

His gaze phlegmatic, Steve sat back and waited. In his experience, most clients viewed their own situation as delicate and problematic. It was something he had come to expect.

Having reached the stage of seeking outside assistance, they often appeared initially reluctant to confide in a stranger.

They didn't like to admit that they were unable to handle matters themselves, be it a question of security, the necessity for some kind of protection, or in finding a missing person.

Steve portrayed an outward veneer of cool professionalism even while his impatience increased. For some reason, besides the wait, something about Mr Apostolakis had rubbed him up the wrong way. He felt wary, vaguely unsettled. But he was careful not to show any emotion.

'Mr Westwood, I am endeavouring to carry out the last wishes of a most important client and to see that the instructions of his will are discharged to the letter.

'I have been unable, so far, to trace one of the main beneficiaries,' the Greek continued, his hands returning to the desk where they fiddled with a dagger-like letter opener. 'Ms Bennett seems to have disappeared.'

'Disappeared?'

'Vanished into thin air,' he clarified

with a dramatic impression of a puff of smoke.

'Perhaps you could fill me in on the steps you have taken so far.'

'But of course.'

With a magnanimous smile, Mr Apostolakis unlocked the centre drawer of his desk and withdrew a file filled to overflowing with papers.

While he waited, Steve took out his notebook and flipped it open on his knee, resisting the temptation to tap the pen impatiently on the paper. Clearly this was going to be a marathon session with Mr Apostolakis taking his own sweet time to set his cards on the table.

'I have very little for you to go on, I'm afraid,' he said, scant apology in his voice. 'Ms Bennett appears to be an impulsive and not entirely responsible young lady.'

'In what way?'

'Disappearing acts have been something of a habit, I think.'

'You mean she's run away before?'

7

The Greek looked uncomfortable, as if he had said something he shouldn't. Steve wondered suddenly if Mr Apostolakis was really in charge or if someone unknown was pulling invisible strings.

No reply to his query was forthcoming however, the only response being a non-committal shrug.

Great, Steve thought. This got better and better. What was he dealing with here, a troublesome teenager? The Greek spoke again, cutting across his thoughts.

'My instructions are simply to employ your company to locate Ms Bennett's whereabouts. We will then make contact with her regarding the terms and conditions of the legacy. You are required to do no more, no less, than that.'

Steve had the impression there was a whole lot more that Mr Apostolakis could not or would not tell him.

'It is a substantial amount of money we are talking about, Mr Westwood.

We have to satisfy ourselves that certain criteria and conditions are met. Discretion is the key.'

'We are always discreet.'

'But of course,' Mr Apostolakis allowed with a small smile. 'I can give you Ms Bennett's last known address.'

'And a picture?'

The Greek shook his head regretfully.

'No picture. Only what I have told you.'

Which wasn't much at all. Steve sighed.

'Could Ms Bennett have gone abroad?'

'No, Mr Westwood. I understand her passport remains in my client's safe. I do not have access at this time.'

Steve frowned, disturbed by the cloak and dagger attitude. The evasive solicitor was not telling him everything. He struggled to keep the shortness from his voice.

'Mr Apostolakis, if we are to help you satisfactorily we need your full co-operation,' Steve contended. 'We can only work with what you give us.'

'I am sure you will do your best. Your agency comes highly recommended.'

Steve sighed and glanced down at the inadequate notes he had been able to jot down in his notebook.

'What about family, friends, anything like that?'

'Let me see.' The Greek's gaze slid away and he made a point of looking through the bulging file. 'Here we are. There is mention of a grandfather who worked here in London at one of the museums.'

'Which one?'

'I'm not sure. It may have been the Victoria and Albert, or perhaps the British.'

'But he doesn't work there now?' Steve asked, envisaging plenty of leg work ahead of him.

Mr Apostolakis gave one of his characteristic shrugs.

'It is my understanding that he has recently retired.'

'I see. You don't happen to have

an address for him, I suppose?' Steve suggested more in hope than expectation, but it was no surprise when the solicitor shook his head. 'And friends of Ms Bennett?'

'There is one I know of. Jillian. Jillian Edwards. She is a fashion model.'

Steve wasn't sure if the disapproval that dripped from the Greek's words was for the profession in general or the young lady in particular. He made some more notes in his book and copied down the address where the elusive Ms Bennett had last resided.

Then he raised his enigmatic grey gaze to meet the cold, brown one.

'And you're sure there is nothing else you can tell me?'

'I regret that is so.'

'Have you tried placing newspaper notices?'

Mr Apostolakis looked shocked.

'I have mentioned the sensitivity, Mr Westwood.'

'It's an avenue usually explored in these cases.'

'One to be attempted in this case only after others have been exhausted.' He took a breath and moderated his tone. 'Now, I shall leave the matter in your hands.'

Pleased to accept the dismissal, Steve rose to his feet. He shook hands briefly, then stepped away, tucking his notebook back into his jacket pocket.

'You will keep me updated on progress, Mr Westwood.'

'Of course. I'll be in touch.'

'Thank you. Goodbye.'

* * *

It had begun to drizzle when Steve stepped back on to the busy London street a few moments later. The light was already beginning to fade and the early March afternoon was cold, offering little promise of spring.

He hailed a taxi and spent the journey back to the agency lost in thought, wondering how much Mr Apostolakis really wanted him to find Ms Bennett.

He had been impossibly cagey and unhelpful. If she couldn't be traced what happened to the money? It was an intriguing thought, but did it in any way explain the man's obstructive behaviour?

He paid the taxi driver and crossed the pavement to their offices, housed in an old, converted house.

The small reception area, spartan in comparison to the one he had come to know that afternoon, was empty when he walked in.

Nodding to one of their new assistants who was on his way out to an early evening assignment, Steve went through the passageway to the back office.

'You've been gone a long time.' Mike greeted him with inappropriate cheerfulness.

Steve glowered at his friend who lounged in the only comfortable chair, his bad leg propped up on cushions.

'I thought you were meant to be resting at home.'

Mike waved the sarcasm aside and

shifted his position.

'How did you get on?'

'You owe me one,' Steve grumbled, wrenching off his tie and loosening the top button of his shirt.

'That bad?'

'Put it this way, if I didn't know better, I'd say you twisted that knee on purpose.'

He cast his partner a sidelong glance.

'Another half an hour and I'd have been tempted to twist the other one for you.'

'So you and Mr Apostolakis really hit it off then, did you?'

Born in Trinidad and raised in the East End of London, Mike had a ready sense of humour and a colourful turn of phrase. He was also intelligent, loyal, and before this afternoon at least, the best friend Steve had.

'He was a real charmer.'

'What's the story?'

Steve made them both a cup of tea and filled his partner in on the appointment, his feelings about the solicitor, and the nature of the job they had been employed to carry out.

'You haven't much to go on,' Mike agreed with an unsympathetic grin. He gestured to his injury and leaned back with lazy unrepentance. 'Shame I'm stuck here, so I can't really help. I wish you luck though.'

Steve picked up a huge pile of accounts and assorted paperwork and dumped it down in the centre of Mike's tidy, organised desk.

'Hey, what's that?' he objected, the grin fading.

Steve smiled innocently, picked up his things and headed for the door.

'Something for you to be going on with while I hunt down our Ms Bennett.'

With Mike's uncomplimentary curse ringing in his ears, Steve sketched a wave and left the office.

2

'Mrs Peterson?' Steve smiled at the elderly lady who stood behind the counter in the deserted, backstreet café. Grey-haired and robust, she faced him, the piercing blue eyes watchful and wary. Her lined, powdered face was unsmiling as he walked across the faded linoleum floor towards her.

'Who wants to know?'

Sitting down, Steve passed her his identification.

'I'm trying to locate a Ms Bennett. I understand she rented an upstairs flat from you.'

'Maybe she did, maybe she didn't,' came the sharp retort. The woman folded her arms across her ample bosom, ignoring his card that sat untouched on the counter top. 'What do you want with her?'

Steve sucked in a breath, surprised

at the tension and hostility his enquiry had unleashed, unsure if Mrs Peterson was anti-Ms Bennett or for some reason protective of her.

'I have some good news for her,' he explained, pressing ahead with caution. 'She has been left an inheritance and the solicitor handling the will has employed my agency to locate her. This is the last address he had.'

He thought he detected the tiniest crack in Mrs Peterson's guard as she digested his words. She glanced down at his card, then her blue gaze returned to his, as she summed him up. Steve faced the inspection openly, his grey eyes clear and without guile.

Mrs Peterson sniffed and turned towards a hissing coffee machine.

'Would you like a cup?'

'I'd love one.'

For a moment she kept her back turned and concentrated on her task, obviously giving herself a few moments for clear thought, Steve allowed. After

17

a minute, the hissing increased to be followed by an alarming splutter. Seconds later, Mrs Peterson set an old-fashioned cup before him containing a milky, unappetising-looking brew.

Steve stared at it for a moment before remembering his manners.

'Thank you.' He smiled, wondering how to drink it.

'That'll be sixty-five pence.'

Steve hid a smile and obediently placed the correct money on the counter. Mrs Peterson hurried the coins away and consigned them to the cash register. Glancing down at the unrecognisable liquid in his cup, he considered the possibility of the food being the same standard as the beverages. He didn't think he'd risk first-hand experience finding out.

'You were going to tell me about Ms Bennett,' he prompted, daring himself to take a sip of coffee.

'I hadn't decided one way or the other.'

The snappy rejoinder momentarily

diverted his attention from the mouthful of liquid he had forced himself to swallow. Even army survival rations hadn't tasted this awful.

'Sugar?' Mrs Peterson asked, sliding the bowl across to him.

'No, thank you,' he declined.

'I can't help you find Lexie, you know.'

Thankful to return to the matter in hand, Steve met the steady blue gaze.

'But she did live here?'

'She did.'

At last they were getting somewhere, but Steve knew he would have to tread carefully to draw Mrs Peterson out.

'What can you tell me about her?'

It was not part of his brief, but any information that could give him an insight into the person he was trying to find could be useful. Although Mrs Peterson believed she did not know anything of value, once she could be persuaded to talk, she may hold clues that would help him pinpoint Lexie Bennett's whereabouts.

'Lexie is a wonderful person,' Mrs Peterson confided with a sigh, the warmth in her voice capturing his attention. 'It makes you feel better just being around her. She sparkles. I can't put it any better than that.'

'You obviously knew her well.' Steve smiled, thankfully pushing his half-empty cup aside.

'Lexie always has time for people, as if they are all really special, you know?'

Steve nodded his understanding. It was quite a character reference, and he doubted if the formidable, old lady was anyone's fool. If she thought so highly of Lexie Bennett, she must have good reason, none of which matched the impression Mr Apostolakis had given him of a troublesome, irresponsible runaway.

'Did she ever mention family to you?'

'Only her grandfather. Her mother died when Lexie was young. I didn't know Lexie then, of course, but she

20

mentioned her mother occasionally. It was her grandparents she doted on. They were very close. She was devastated when her grandmother passed away a couple of years ago. It was a bad time for her.'

Mrs Peterson tutted at the memory, then a smile lifted her dour expression.

'Her grandfather retired soon after. He's a Scot, from Ayr, I think Lexie said. Somewhere thereabouts. She was always talking about Scotland. She spent holidays there with her grandparents and loved it. She and Jillian went up together once or twice.'

'Her model friend?'

'That's right. Something of a madam that one, but they were as thick as thieves. Went to some fancy boarding school together.'

Steve folded his arms and leaned against the counter.

'Where was that?' he asked casually, not wanting to disturb Mrs Peterson now she was in full flow.

'Heavens, I don't know. I don't think Lexie ever mentioned the name.'

'When did you last see her?'

The blue eyes clouded.

'Nearly a year ago now. Cried buckets I did when she left. Such a sweet lass. I'm sorry, I really can't tell you any more.'

'I'm grateful for your time.'

Steve smiled as he stood up.

'You've been very helpful.'

'I've enjoyed reminiscing about her,' Mrs Peterson admitted with a rare smile in return. 'Of course, I didn't tell any of this to the other people who were looking for her . . . '

Steve hesitated on the walk to the door, suddenly tense.

'What other people?'

'A while ago it was now. Foreigners. Rude they were and a sight too pushy for my liking. I didn't take to them, didn't think they were up to any good.'

'What did they say?'

'They wouldn't say what they wanted her for, or why they needed to know where she was. I didn't tell them anything. Said I never spoke to her much, that I knew nothing.' Mrs Peterson sniffed derisively. ' 'I keeps to meself,' I told them. Guess it was wrong to lie, but I didn't trust them. Nor did I want them giving Lexie any bother. Have to go with your instincts, don't you?'

'Yes.'

Steve gave her an encouraging smile, inwardly digesting the new information. He knew all about instincts. Could it be he was right to feel there was more behind the request to find Lexie Bennett. But what? And how was he going to find out?

'I guess you're all right,' Mrs Peterson continued. 'She has an inheritance you say?' She laughed aloud. 'Doubt that will concern Lexie none. She'd never bothered much about money. Never fussed after things for herself, but always helps others. Heart of gold that girlie has. If you find her, tell her I think of her. I miss her bright and caring ways about the place.'

'I will.' Steve hesitated a moment longer. 'You were so close, I'm surprised she never told you where she was going, that she didn't keep in touch.'

'Oh, I hear from her.'

'What? But you said — '

'I don't know where she is, but she sends me cards, at Christmas, never forgets my birthday or the anniversary my husband died. I can never make out these postmarks and I never know where to reply to. I'd love to see her again. I'm sorry,' she broke off with an embarrassed shrug. 'You must think I'm a rambling, old woman.'

'Not at all.'

Steve was touched that his target had made such an impression and brought cheer to the lonely woman's life. It seemed his Ms Bennett was a caring, unselfish person. So how could someone like that have run away, worried the people who cared about her, left no trace of her whereabouts? It didn't make any sense.

His next stop was the museum, and he was lucky to pick the right one first time. But that was only because it was closer, he allowed with a wry smile. It didn't take him long to discover that Alisdair Bennett had indeed retired from his job at the museum.

He had lived in a small house a few streets away, but had moved now and left no forwarding address. It was becoming a familiar picture. One member of staff thought it possible he had returned to Scotland.

Not much to go on, Steve mused, but he checked out Mr Bennett's old address just the same.

None of the neighbours could help him. Either they had moved in since, or were unable to remember anything of any use. People came and went and very little notice was taken.

In the afternoon, he followed up a lead he had on Jillian Edwards, the fashion model friend. A few calls had located the agency she was registered with and a bit of sweet-talk had illicited the information that Jillian was currently working in a small charity show at a local store.

Steve was thankful it was nearly over when he arrived. Fashion shows were not his thing, and nor were models. A few discreet questions soon pointed him in the direction of a tall, reed-thin redhead.

Interest flared in clear, green eyes when he approached, and he fought down a wave of tired annoyance as he recognised the open invitation in their depths.

'Jillian Edwards?'

She sent him a coy smile before she answered his query.

'I hoped you were looking for me. It must be my lucky day.'

'Actually,' he said, ignoring the signals, 'I'm looking for Lexie.'

'Sorry.' The green eyes turned glacial. 'I don't know where she is.'

'I find that hard to believe. You're best friends.'

'At school we were.'

'And since.'

'I haven't seen her in a long time. Excuse me, please.'

'I thought you'd been together in Scotland.'

Steve watched the sudden shock and alarm flash across the girl's face. It had been a risk, but his tactic had paid off, told him what he wanted to know.

'You're mistaken,' she said coldly, recovering her composure quickly. 'I can't help you.'

As she spun on her heel and walked away to join the other models, Steve watched her. She was older than he had expected, but that was probably all the make up she had been wearing.

Jillian glanced back and saw him looking at her, a mixture of mistrust and uncertainty on her face. He wondered why Jillian, like Mrs Peterson, thought it necessary to protect Lexie Bennett. From what? From whom?

Back at his desk, Steve cleared up some urgent paperwork, but his mind was on the information he had assimilated that day. He sighed and leaned back in his chair.

Something about this case had sparked his interest. So many things were at odds, and quite frankly, the more he discovered about Ms Lexie Bennett, the more intrigued he became.

He knew what he had to do. All the signposts were pointing towards Scotland.

3

Global warming may be a world problem, Lexie allowed, but it seemed to be having little effect in this isolated Scottish glen. She let herself out of the cottage and faced another frosty morning. It had been a bitterly cold spring so far. Snow lingered on the hills and only the most hardy individuals had begun walking in the area and along the Southern Upland Way.

They were seeing a few of them now in the pub at lunchtimes and in the evenings — cold, wet, but fiercely determined. A hearty meal, a couple of drinks and some friendly local chat had seen them on their way again.

Lexie pulled her hat down tighter over her riot of ebony curls that fell in a gleaming mass halfway to her waist. Then she thrust her gloved hands deeper into the pockets of her heavy, wool jacket. She shivered at the thought of the brisk walk ahead of her along the deserted lane towards the village a couple of miles away.

It had been welcome to receive a lift home the night before when fog had descended, but it had meant leaving her bicycle behind at the pub. How she would appreciate it now to speed her arrival. She thought longingly of the roaring log fires Ross would by now have burning in all the grates.

An unusually hard and persistent winter had followed a long, hot summer and lingering, bright autumn. The heather had coloured the hills and the rich reds and browns had followed on throughout November and into December.

She had been told that in previous years the winters had been kind, only some hard frosts and isolated flurries of snow to show for the time of year. The worst of the weather had been above the Glasgow-Edinburgh line.

But this was her first winter. She had

seen their corner of Scotland, Burns country in the Ayrshire, Dumfries and Border districts, hit by heavy snow and freezing weather.

A crisp, white blanket had cloaked the glen, all but sealing her in on more than one occasion in her farm cottage, which she rented from the local landowner.

Despite the severity of the season, it had been beautiful, Lexie allowed with a smile. The morning exercise took the chill from her body, her warm breath forming regular puffs of cloud in the cold air.

Her tiny cottage, nestled in the trees beside the burn in the mouth of the glen, had been covered in snow for weeks.

Only a slushy patch round the hot spot of the chimney revealed any signs of thaw. The trees themselves, stark and dormant, had taken on new shapes as snow had settled, tracing out each branch and twig.

She had been feeding the birds for

the whole of the winter, and had been rewarded with an array of colourful visitors. The most prized was a great spotted woodpecker who had been a regular caller as the weeks went on.

It had been enjoyable to watch them, feathers fluffed up against the cold, and she liked to think her little garden had been an oasis in the surrounding bleakness.

Now the birds, still hungry, were beginning to have faith in the arrival of spring. The dark roof of the cottage, spattered with patches of lichen, was showing again above the mellow blocks of the walls.

Melt water from the hills had swelled the burn which ran fast to join the river, pounding over rocks and tumbling down the waterfall where she had seen salmon leaping on their journey to the spawning grounds upstream the previous autumn.

She loved it here, Lexie admitted as the village came into view. It was in stark contrast from the life she had known in London. Her occasional trips up to Glasgow to collect her mail from her post office box had shown her that she could never again live in the hustle and bustle, the noise and anonymity of a big city.

For nearly a year she had enjoyed this life. She had begun to settle and believe she was free to stop looking over her shoulder. An anxious frown creased her brow. But the postcard that had been amongst the mail she had picked up yesterday had filled her with new doubts and concern.

The card had been advertising a new range of fashion wear. Scrawled across it had been the invitation to 'Be Someone New', and on the back, unsigned but in recognisable handwriting in the code they had made up for fun at boarding school, the message she had transcribed as, *careful, asking, questions*.

To anyone else, it wouldn't make sense, but put together, Jillian's warning, dated only a few days ago, had come through loud and clear.

Be careful, someone is asking new questions.

Lexie let herself into the welcoming warmth of the pub, a feeling of dread weighing heavily in the pit of her stomach. Despite all her efforts, it was happening again.

★ ★ ★

'Mike, I think I have a positive lead on Lexie Bennett.'

Steve leaned his shoulder against the side of the draughty telephone box and looked out across the Firth of Clyde to the domed lump of Ailsa Craig.

'That was fast work,' his partner complimented.

'I got lucky. I played a hunch and it came off.'

'Where are you?'

'Girvan — south of Ayr, Scotland,' he added with a grin, knowing how rarely Mike acknowledged anything north of the London metropolis.

A derisive snort greeted his sarcastic teasing.

'Gee, thanks. Tell me what's happened so far.'

Steve gave him a summary of his activities since taking the train from London to Carlisle three days ago, where he picked up a hire car. He had drawn a blank in Ayr initially, which was hardly surprising. There hadn't been much to work on.

About to give up, a flash of inspiration had turned him in the direction of the local cultural centres and places of historical interest.

He figured that a man who had been gainfully employed in a field that fascinated him would find it hard to let go when he retired. Where better to channel that interest and energy than by volunteering his services at one of the many tourist sites that dotted the area in honour of Scotland's national poet, Robert Burns?

It had meant some touring around, and that had taken time, but he had hit the jackpot yesterday afternoon. Alisdair Bennett did indeed spend some of his time involved in a local museum, and it had not taken Steve long to discover that he lived in Girvan.

From there, he had soon managed to locate the place, but not Mr Bennett. A few drinks at a local tavern, where he had posed as an old acquaintance from London, had furnished him with the information that there was indeed a grand-daughter who worked in a pub in a village some miles inland.

'So that's where you're going next?' Mike asked when Steve completed his report. 'You're not going to wait to see Mr Bennett himself?'

'I don't see the point. If the lead pans out and it is Lexie, I won't need to bother the grandfather at all.' Steve paused for a moment as he considered his plan. 'The village is a stopping post on the Southern Upland Way, a natural break for hikers. I thought I'd walk in, as I just happen to have brought my gear with me! It will look less suspicious than rolling up in a hire car and asking questions.'

'Sure! Like you ever turn down the opportunity of some exercise and a good hike.'

'Exactly.' Steve laughed. 'Shame about that knee of yours.'

He put down the receiver, chuckling to himself at Mike's parting retort. With Mike wanting to spend as much time as possible with his young family, it had naturally developed that Steve had taken on any travelling that would entail time away from home. He made what use of it he could.

He had never expected to wrap up this job so quickly — had hardly imagined ever being within reach of Lexie Bennett after the unhelpful brief Mr Apostolakis had given him. As it was, he could spend an enjoyable couple of days confirming he had indeed located her, then he could be on his way home.

If all went well, he could even snatch

a visit with his family in Nottingham on the way.

It would mean some rerouting, but it would be worth it. He saw his parents and his elder brother and sister far too seldom, what with army life and then the pressures and time-consuming effort getting the agency on its feet.

Pleased with the way the Bennett case was coming together, Steve went back to the car and drove to the village where he would pick up the Southern Upland Way. With luck, by this time tomorrow he would have good news to relate to Mr Apostolakis.

★ ★ ★

Had she been careful enough, Lexie worried, turning away from the bar as she measured a double whisky into a glass for one of the lunchtime regulars.

Despite being busy and occupied with her work all morning, she had been conscious of a growing unease and concern at Jillian's cryptic message.

38

She served the drink with a smile, determined none of her new friends and acquaintances would see how troubled she was.

She had thought for a long time about this move. It had been planned with stealth and care, even as the faint hope had remained that it would never be necessary to do it. That hope had perished, but her foresight had been a lifesaver.

She had moved on, adjusted, carved a new life for herself in this Scottish Borders village. Most importantly, she had covered her tracks — or so she had thought. Even, white teeth chewed her lower lip. She wished she knew more of the circumstances that had prompted Jillian to send her the warning.

During a rare slack moment in the bar, she thought back over the last year. It had been a difficult time, but she had embraced the challenge, the new experiences, and made new friends. She refused to look back and wouldn't allow herself regrets.

But could all her efforts and planning have been in vain? Surely it couldn't all be happening again. She had made her bid for freedom and she would fight anyone who tried to take it from her.

'Lexie?'

Ross MacBride's mellow-accented voice interrupted her reverie and she turned to find her employer peering at her through the order hatch that led to the kitchen.

He was a middle-aged, jocular, red-haired giant of a man and his family had run this pub, the best for miles around, for the last five decades.

'Yes, boss?' Lexie smiled at him.

'Old Mrs Stewart along the High Street is ill. She's just rung to ask me to run some soup along for her,' Ross explained as he pulled on his woolly jacket. 'Hold the fort in the kitchen for a wee while.'

'Of course. Would you rather I went for you?'

'Oh, no,' he declined with a smile,

jamming a cap on his head. A teasing glint entered his light green eyes. 'You're so soft you'll be stuck running errands and we won't see you for hours. She knows she can't take advantage of me!'

The outer door to the main street opened and a gust of cold air blew in, fluttering the flames in the grates and stirring a pile of paper napkins on one corner of the bar. Lexie glanced up from the order pad to view the new arrival.

She didn't recognise this man, who appeared to be in his early thirties. She watched as he read the notice in the porch and bent to remove his muddy boots. Another walker. Lexie glanced away and confirmed a lunch order before serving the hungry customers with drinks.

From the corner of her eye, she watched as the hiker crossed in socked feet to a vacant table near one of the fires. He shrugged out of his rucksack, then took off his waterproof jacket and draped it on a chair to dry near the flames.

He was of medium height, hard and fit, his face attractive, lean and masculine. His cheeks were faintly coloured from the chill wind and exertion. As he glanced around the bar, he pushed up the sleeves of his heavy cream jumper, then ran the fingers of one hand through his damp, wayward hair.

Lexie shook her head ruefully at her uncharacteristic inspection of the stranger. After serving the drinks she had prepared, she left Andy, an efficient and friendly young man, in charge of the bar, and went through to the kitchen to help with the lunch orders.

Steve sipped his beer, the warmth of the log fire easing the chill from his bones. He looked around the inn and felt comfortable with the friendly ambience and the rustic style.

The walk had blown away some of the city cobwebs. Any free time he had he took to the hills. He loved the freedom, the exercise, the solitude of the wide open spaces, and some of the country he had been through that morning had been breathtaking, even through the drizzle.

It was not an area he had visited before and he wished he had more time to explore the snow-capped hills, the paths and tracks still mushy and water-logged from the thaw. But he could not ignore his responsibilities. He was here to work.

From the general chatter, he assessed that most of the customers in the bar were locals, either enjoying a relaxing lunch hour, or older folk meeting friends and enjoying the company. His gaze moved on, searching for a girl who could be Lexie Bennett.

At that moment, a teenager, blonde and waif-like, came through a swing door from the kitchen carrying two plates of sandwiches. Was this the quarry he had come so far to find?

He watched her as she walked to the other side of the room and set down the food, offering a shy smile to the customers before she retreated to the kitchen.

His mouth formed a faint pout of concentration. Had she looked like the girl who had run away, who had endeared herself to Mrs Peterson, who had inspired such loyalty in her friends? Steve could not tell. He would endeavour to discover her identity when she brought his lunch from the bar.

A few moments later, the blonde teenager emerged from the kitchen once more and headed in his direction. As if aware of his inspection, the girl looked up as she approached the table, a flush staining her pale cheeks as she met his speculative gaze.

His attention appeared to make her nervous and Steve frowned as she became clumsy, the basket of rolls and bowl of soup she was bringing him catching the edge of the table and spilling to the carpeted floor.

'Oh!' she exclaimed, embarrassment

flaming her cheeks once more as she tried to mop up the mess. 'I'm so sorry.'

'Don't worry about it.'

Steve bent down to gather up the scattered rolls as she picked up the crockery. Before he could question her, she took the basket from him and backed towards the kitchen.

'I'll get you some fresh,' she murmured before she turned and fled.

★ ★ ★

Lexie glanced up from preparing a ploughman's platter as a flustered Christine hurried in and clattered dishes and a handful of crushed rolls on to the drainer.

'Are you all right?'

'I've just made a complete idiot of myself.'

The younger girl grimaced.

'And I all but threw the soup at the poor man. It went all over, but he was nice about it.'

45

Lexie sighed and gave her a sympathetic smile.

'What happened?'

'He flustered me, staring all the time.' She glanced pleadingly at Lexie. 'I can't go back out there. I'll have to wait until I feel a bit less nervous.'

Lexie hid a flash of exasperation. They couldn't cope today if Christine had a sudden attack of the vapours. They had a lot of staff off sick and Ross's wife was also ill in their flat upstairs.

'All right,' she conceded.

She finished the lunch she was preparing and served it at the bar counter. A sigh of relief escaped as she returned to the kitchen and saw Ross appearing at the back door.

He could supervise Christine in the kitchen, she acknowledged as she prepared another bowl of soup and basket of rolls.

'Which table is this for?'

Christine sent her a grateful smile. 'Seven. But believe me, you can't possibly miss him!'

Lexie shook her head. Christine may be a hard worker and excellent when it came to food preparation, but she was still young and skittish, and far too liable to have her mind wander when faced with interest from the opposite sex.

She smiled to herself as she left the kitchen and crossed to the appointed table, realising it was occupied by the walker she had noticed on his arrival a while ago.

'I'm sorry about the problems,' she apologised as she set the bowl of steaming homemade soup before him and put down the basket of rolls.

Intent, ash-grey eyes regarded her for a moment, then his mouth curved in a smile.

'It's just one of those things,' Steve said gently.

'Are you on holiday?' she enquired in friendly fashion as she wiped away the last of the mess Christine had made.

'Just enjoying a few days' walking.'

The deep warmth of his voice surprised her.

'Not the best weather for you.' She smiled as she straightened and encountered that gaze once more.

'I don't mind the rain. It's a beautiful area.'

'Yes, it is.' Lexie swallowed. When he smiled that way she felt a little jolt inside her. 'I — '

'Lexie?'

She glanced round as Andy called her from behind the bar and nodded to him in acknowledgement.

Surprised at the disconcerted expression on the walker's face as she looked back at him, she noticed the frown that pulled the straight brows together. And his attractive smile had faded. She shrugged aside the feeling that something had upset him.

'Please excuse me, we are short staffed today,' she explained, sending him a warm smile. 'Enjoy your meal.'

As she walked away, the flutter in her stomach failed to dissipate. It was ridiculous, but she felt as if an image of that handsome face and those compelling, steel-grey eyes had somehow been branded on her brain.

She could feel his gaze on her now.

No matter how she tried to laugh it off or drive the sensation away, a tingle fluttered along her spine.

He was an attractive man, but only one of many she had seen in her life. So why did she feel that instant awareness, the magnetic tug? Disconcerted, she forced herself not to look at him again, not to give in to the overwhelming urge she had to return to his table and talk to him some more.

Come on, Lexie, she lectured herself as she approached the bar. Pull yourself together.

4

That exotic-looking creature was Lexie Bennett? Steve was unable to take his gaze off her. As she walked away from him, her swirling skirt in fire engine red swung around her, and the bright, fluffy jumper she wore, rich with a multitude of colours heightened her vibrancy.

Olive-skinned, with dark, laughing eyes, she had hair the colour of jet and so much of it. Thick and lustrous, it fell around her shoulders and down her back in a riot of soft curls.

The surprise at discovering her identity had not worn off. Speaking with her before he had known who she was had allowed him to form an initial opinion unbiased by what he had been told about her.

For a start, she was older. In her early twenties, he judged, and not at all the flighty, truculent teenager Mr Apostolakis had implied. Indeed, she had been warm and friendly and from what he had seen, she was clearly responsible and intelligent.

None of which matched the picture the solicitor had given him. Why? The further he went with this case, the more wary he felt.

As Lexie finished talking to the barman and went back to the kitchen, Steve forced himself to turn his attention to his lunch. He felt confused, almost stunned, and he did not want to examine the immediate impact the colourful and vital Ms Bennett had made upon him.

There had been a buzz of unexpected excitement when he had been speaking with her. But he should be able to ignore the awareness. And now, as warmth curled inside him, he knew it wasn't from the infusion of the still-steaming soup.

When he finished his lunch, he pushed his plate aside and sat back, warming his toes by the fire.

Much of the lunchtime rush was over, many of the customers had gone and Lexie was back behind the bar. He adjusted his chair so he could watch her more easily. It was no surprise to him that a couple of men had lingered to talk to her, attracted like moths to a flame. Not that she flirted or teased, Steve noticed. Far from it.

She was natural, vivacious, the kind of woman whose appeal was born from within. Her beauty was more to do with soul, personality, than with outward packaging. She was the kind of woman a man could fall hard for.

One young man in mechanics overalls was gazing at her from farther down the counter with spaniel-like devotion, clearly smitten. While the smile she bestowed on him was kind and under-standing, there was no invitation or encouragement. Steve felt sorry for him . . . and relieved.

This is ridiculous, he chastised himself, cursing the fact that he found her so captivating. He didn't even know the woman.

Not only that but he was here to do a job. Only now the job was done. Over. He had found Ms Lexie Bennett. He could go home, make his report, claim his fee, and forget all about her.

He swallowed down a sudden inner protest and rose to his feet with a burst of exasperation. What on earth was the matter with him?

'You get off home, Lexie. You deserve a well-earned break,' Ross instructed when the rush had passed and the clearing up from lunch was complete. 'I can cope until this evening.'

Lexie glanced at him. She couldn't deny she would welcome the three or so hours to unwind before the night shift. The extra time she had worked in the last ten days had begun to sap her energy reserves, but that was the same for all of them while they were short-staffed. Even so, she didn't like leaving Ross to handle everything himself.

'Are you sure?' she queried with concern. 'I don't mind staying.'

'I know, and I don't know what I would have done without you. You're a treasure. But Andy is staying an extra couple of hours and Jim is back tonight which will relieve the pressure for the rest of us. No, you take some time, Lexie,' he finished, the stern insistence of his tone offset by a grateful smile.

Lexie nodded her acceptance and returned the smile before she finished washing the glasses then dried her hands. As she walked to the staff room to collect her things, she cast a glance at the almost empty bar.

The walker's table was vacant. One moment he had been sitting by the fire, relaxed and replete after his lunch, that disturbing grey gaze watching her and warming her blood, and then, feeling a strange sense of loss, she had looked round and he had gone. Just like that.

She still felt the unaccountable sting of regret. And no matter how much she told herself it was best if she put him from her mind, it was proving easier said than done.

With a sigh, she wrapped up, wedged her hat precariously on her mass of ebony curls, and let herself out of the back door and crossed the cobbled yard to unchain her bicycle from the railings.

It was still cold but the cloud had lifted, taking with it the drizzle. The sun was now making a tentative effort to brighten the rest of the day.

As she rode down the main street towards the turn-off for the glen, she waved absently to Gordon Robertson, the garage mechanic. He was back at work after his regular weekday sandwich in the bar. He spent most of his lunchtimes endeavouring without success to chat her up.

She liked him, enjoyed his company, but like most of the men she had met since she had moved, she felt no romantic attraction.

She had a varied social life but so far,

nothing had gone beyond friendship.

Now, with a sudden uncertainty of her position here, she was relieved she was emotionally unencumbered. If she had to move again in a hurry, it was as well to have no ties to break.

Even at that, it would be difficult to leave her new friends, her job, this village. She loved it here. Lexie sighed. She did not want to be forced to move on. Not again. And when would it stop?

With her thoughts once more weighing heavily on her mind, she pedalled home.

★ ★ ★

As Steve came out of the village shop and wedged the chocolate bars he had bought into a pocket of his rucksack, he glanced along the street and saw Lexie Bennett pedal her bicycle out of the pub carpark. Even wrapped up in a thick wool jacket with a large, felt hat on her head, he would have known her

56

anywhere. No-one else he had ever seen had hair like that.

He watched her cycle away from him down the main street, wave a greeting to someone and then turn down a narrow lane. Hitching his rucksack into a comfortable position, he set off in the same direction.

According to his ordnance map he had studied some time before, the route she had taken had only one destination. The glen. It was almost his route back to the Southern Upland Way, the trail that would take him to the neighbouring village where he had left the hire car.

He should go straight home, make his report, and forget all about her, he told himself again.

A long sigh escaped and he dragged his fingers through his thick, breeze-tousled hair. But he didn't want to do that.

At least he could talk to her again after he had come all this way to find her, and he was bound to see her somewhere along the lane. There was nowhere else to go.

What harm could it do to see her again? He could confirm her identity, break the news about her good fortune, satisfy this curiosity about her that had crept up on him.

Besides, although he couldn't say precisely what it was that bothered him, he felt an urge to ensure that things were above board before he felt he could complete his report on this assignment.

Something about Mr Apostolakis, the whole brief, and then the reactions of Mrs Peterson and Jillian Edwards, made him wary. He still thought there was more going on than he had been told. And Lexie herself was not at all that he expected.

Now he had the opportunity to put his mind at rest before he passed anything to Mr Apostolakis. Surely that was a good reason to talk to her? Of course it was.

That it could be anything to do with

the instant impact Lexie had made on him, Steve did not want to think about.

Walking down the lane with an easy, deceptive stride, half his mind was on his thoughts.

The other half acknowledged the beauty of the scenery, the closing in of the spectacular hills, the appearance of the sun and the promise of spring to come. Lexie Bennett had certainly found herself a beautiful spot to live.

A frown creased his brow. Why was she here, in this isolated spot? It was miles from the grandfather she doted on and had chosen to follow to Scotland. And it was a stark contrast from her city life in London. The more he thought, the more questions he had.

For instance, why she had apparently been at pains to cover her tracks, and why her friends either didn't know where she was or pretended not to. He was both intrigued and troubled. There were many things about this whole business that didn't add up.

Although he had only walked a couple of miles, he already felt he was out in the wilds.

He had passed a few cottages near the village, and one large farm almost a mile back, but other than that, there was no sign of human presence. Where on earth had Lexie been going? Had he missed her?

The only sounds that disturbed the peace of the glen were the occasional cries of a buzzard, a few small birds going about their business, and the music of the tumbling water that bubbled over rocks and boulders in the burn that edged the lane.

Steve passed through a gate beside a cattle grid, rounded a bend in the lane and then he saw a pair of remote cottages nestled amongst a stand of windshaped trees. One looked empty, bleak and cold, but the other was clearly inhabited.

Smoke curled from the terracotta chimney pot that rose from the slate roof. Bright, flowery curtains hung in the windows and pots of plants nestled on the sills behind the tiny panes of glass.

A bicycle was propped up against the mellow stone wall. Lexie's bike. Steve hesitated by the wooden gate, lingering, undecided.

Before he could make up his mind whether to make his presence known or retreat unnoticed and be on his way, Lexie appeared round the side of the cottage carrying a load of logs.

When she saw him she jumped in surprise, and several logs tumbled from her grasp and spilled haphazardly on to the path.

Steve almost convinced himself that he had imagined the look of distress that clouded her dark eyes before a smile of recognition, or was it relief, banished it. He was almost convinced himself, but not quite.

Had she been anxious that someone else would appear at her gate? Who? Why? The momentary lapse in her self-confident, friendly air both surprised and concerned him.

For several seconds he stared at her, unable to help himself. He was warmed by the smile that now curved the generous bow of her mouth, her anxiety forgotten.

He marvelled again at her hair, the way it seemed to float around her like a thundercloud. Getting a grip on both his manners and his senses, he walked through the gate and helped her gather up the logs.

'I didn't mean to startle you,' he apologised as he straightened and juggled a pile of rough-sawn logs he had collected into a more stable position. There it was again, that smile that tied his insides in knots. He swallowed and dragged his gaze away. 'Where shall I put these for you?'

Lexie responded to the man's query by indicating an empty bin that stood inside the porch.

As he went to unload the logs, she watched him and endeavoured to pull herself together and recover from the initial shock she had experienced at the sight of someone unexpected lurking by the gate.

She had been so engrossed in her thoughts that just for a moment, she thought they had found her.

She had felt a burst of fear and despair before welcome relief had washed over her as she recognised the walker from the pub.

This was all perfectly innocent, she told herself, taking several deep breaths and trying to calm her racing pulse.

He was obviously on his way back to the footpath to continue his walk. There was nothing sinister about his arrival.

'Thank you.' She smiled as the man took the logs she still held in her arms and dropped them into the bin. 'You're off on your walk again?'

He nodded, seemingly in no hurry to be on his way.

'This is such a beautiful place. Have you been here long?' he asked, his gaze sweeping across the landscape.

'A while,' Lexie allowed, forcing herself not to read more into his questions than was there.

'I was surprised to see so much snow on the peaks. Did you have a hard winter here?'

'Very much so.' She smiled and told him about the snow, the ice that had coated the windows, how beautiful it had all been despite the hardship and the freezing temperatures. 'I had never experienced such cold before.'

'Quite a shock to the system, I know.'

'Oh?'

'I was in the army for a few years,' he explained, easing his rucksack off and resting it beside him. 'We did some Arctic training. I wouldn't fancy doing it again, it was pretty unpleasant.'

His eyes crinkled at the corners when he smiled, Lexie noticed. Those smoky grey eyes were at once warm, yet watchful and alert. The awareness she had been conscious of while talking to him in the bar returned with a vengeance, disconcerting her.

She enjoyed meeting people and was normally outgoing, but she felt strangely shy and tongue-tied with this man.

'Is the adjoining cottage unoccupied?' he asked after a moment's silence.

'The local landowner who rents me this half hires it out for holiday lets.'

Since moving here from London, she had felt safer and consequently had become less cautious. But she was here alone and however attractive, friendly and well-mannered, this man was still a stranger. Even as she told herself it was her anxieties playing on her mind after Jillian's warning, she felt a sudden flicker of nervousness.

'Well,' she said, wary and yet fighting an inner reluctance to say goodbye to him, 'thanks for your help with the logs. I expect you want to get back on the trail.'

'Yes.'

She backed up towards the porch, absently flicking wayward strands of long, wavy hair away from her face.

Still he hesitated. Their gazes locked. Lexie felt a heightened tension, sensed an uncertainty in him, as if he wanted to say something else. Unsettled by his effect on her, she made herself turn away, then reached out to open the front door.

'Lexie, wait.'

She froze. Her heart started to hammer against her ribs. How had he known her name? Had he just heard it in the pub, or . . . ? She didn't want to think there was another possibility.

Again she felt a shiver of fear. Slowly, her hands clenching to fists with her tension, she turned back to face him.

5

Steve's senses snapped to attention when Lexie turned round. He could see the anxiety, the thread of fear, return to her dark, luminous eyes.

He had decided to tell her who he was and that he had been unable to keep up the pretence any longer, even though it was not part of his brief to approach her. But her reaction to his use of her name puzzled him.

'Who are you? What do you want?'

He detected the quiver in her voice and saw the way her gaze wavered. He read her tension, noticing how her smile faltered and became frayed around the edges before disappearing altogether. He hated to see her vibrancy in any way diminished.

It brought out an unexpected protective streak in him and he was anxious to reassure her.

'It's OK, honestly, I don't mean any harm. My name is Steve Westwood.'

Slowly, he eased a business card out of his rucksack and handed it across to her. He tried to ignore the way her fingers trembled as she took it, but he could not fail to be aware of her distress as she read the details on the card. He watched the light fade in her eyes when she looked back at him.

He felt at a loss as to why she was so unsettled and alarmed. The silence grew between them.

Steve thrust his hands into his pockets and adopted what he hoped was an unthreatening stance.

'I was hired to trace you,' he explained softly, neither his smile nor his words bringing any response. 'It's good news.'

He was surprised when Lexie gave a cynical half-laugh at his announcement. She shook her head and pressed her fingers to her temples as if in sudden pain.

Steve swallowed and tried again.

'I'm sorry, I didn't mean to alarm you in any way, but . . . Look, can we please talk? Will you allow me to explain?'

For several moments he thought she would refuse. Her dark gaze briefly clashed with his, then dropped away again. Her expression both serious and sorrowful, she turned and opened the door.

'I suppose you had better come in.'

To give herself time to think, Lexie left her unwelcome visitor removing his boots in the porch and went through to her neat, bright, but tiny kitchen to put on the kettle.

She could hardly believe that he was here. She had been found and her year of peace and happiness had effectively come to an end.

The possibility of discovery had hung over her like a spectre, but as time had gone on the threat had appeared to diminish.

She had even begun to relax, push it to the back of her mind. She saw now that she had been both complacent and foolish to imagine they would allow themselves to be outwitted, especially when they had so much at stake.

Perhaps it had been a mistake to put down tentative roots in one place rather than move around.

She had discussed the possibilities with her grandfather. Dear Gramps. More than anything she wanted to see him more often and to be able to live an ordinary life. But he was concerned for her, too, and they had planned her course of action together.

Now they would have to re-plan — again. Because time was running out, and desperate people took desperate steps to get what they wanted. Lexie was more determined than ever that they would be disappointed.

Lexie heard the inner porch door close, and the sound of soft footsteps in the main downstairs room. She poured boiling water into the pot, put it on a tray with a jug of milk, bowl of sugar and two cups, and carried it through.

Steve turned from admiring the view from the window and smiled. She didn't respond. Lexie didn't want to notice how attractive he looked or acknowledge that she was still so aware of him.

He was here, invading her sanctuary, bringing with him a world she had wanted to leave behind.

'Tea?' she asked, her voice controlled, almost abrupt.

'Thank you. Milk, no sugar, please.'

She gestured for him to sit down in one of the two comfortable armchairs that faced the comforting log fire. After pouring the tea, she took the vacant chair, and stared at the flames for several moments. She could feel his gaze on her as she tried to decide how to handle the situation. She glanced up and met the steady grey gaze.

'What do I have to do to persuade you not to give away my whereabouts to anyone?'

She could see she had surprised him. He had been in the process of raising his cup to his mouth but now he slowly set it back on the table.

'Why don't you want to be found?'

'Because I choose not to be.'

'Why?'

'I think that's my business, Mr Westwood.'

Lexie sipped her tea and let him ponder on that for a while. She wished he would back off and just accept her wish to be left alone. Of course, she had no idea what he had been told or exactly why it was that he required to find her. She looked at him through lowered lashes.

If it became necessary, she would tell him just enough to make him see he had probably been misled and that she had cause to remain here undiscovered. Perhaps then he would go away and keep her secret.

Could she convince him? Could she trust him?

Steve leaned back in his chair, outwardly relaxed. Lexie intrigued him. He watched her now trying to act casually, as if she hadn't a care in the world. But however much she hid her gaze from him, she couldn't disguise the play of emotions across her face, nor her tension and concern.

He wanted to know more about her . . . all there was to know. There was something going on here, he was sure of it — something deeper behind his search for her and why she did not want him to give her away. But what? Why was she so anxious, so insistent? He decided to push a bit more.

'I've been employed to do a job and unless you can give me a very good reason why I shouldn't make my report, I'm obligated to my client to give him what he's paying for.'

'And I have no right to privacy?'

How could he argue with that? It was something he understood well. She was tense again now, the dark gaze guarded as she looked at him, resistant and uncertain. He tried a different tack.

'There is a simple reason that will

be beneficial for you as to why my client wants to contact you,' he told her and watched her neat brows lift towards her wispy fringe in sardonic amusement. 'You seem cynical.'

'Do I?'

'I'd like to know, why did you disappear without a word?'

She set her cup on the table and reached out to add another log to the dying fire

'I'm twenty-four-years old, Mr Westwood, and I don't have to ask anyone's permission to do anything.'

Which put him in his place, Steve thought wryly, hiding a smile as admiration for this spirited woman increased.

She had a sharp mind and a strong will and now he was more determined than ever to learn her mysteries.

There were so many contrasts. The watch she wore was expensive, but she lived simply in this tiny cottage that although feminine and homely was not far off rustic.

Her clothes were colourful and she had a style of her own, but they were off-the-peg and he sensed an air of refined breeding about her — a grace and confidence that he sensed was at odds with the person he saw. She had attended a fancy boarding school, yet had lived until the last year in Mrs Peterson's non-descript studio flat.

She had moved from the city of London to this Scottish glen where she travelled by bicycle and worked in the local pub. He found her an enigma.

'I understand my client is talking about a considerable sum that could be due to you,' he expanded, wondering how she would react.

Perhaps what Mrs Peterson had told him about a disinterest in money was true.

'Is money important to you, Mr Westwood?'

'Steve,' he invited, wanting to hear her melodious, sultry voice say his name. 'Not particularly, no.'

'Nor to me.' Lexie allowed a small smile.

'The will — '

'I'm not interested,' she told him with a burst of angry exasperation. 'I know the contents and conditions of my father's will, and — '

'Your father's will?' he interrupted, unable to conceal his surprise.

'What did Yannis say to you, anyway? I presume it was he who hired you, Yannis Apostolakis?'

For the second time in less than a minute, Steve was taken aback.

'Yes,' he confirmed, his mind buzzing with the information as he watched Lexie push a mass of wayward curls behind her shoulder.

'Tell me, do you always believe what your clients tell you?'

'Until I have reason to believe otherwise.'

The dark gaze locked with his.

'And if I give you reason?'

'Can you?'

Steve watched her for a moment, his distrust of Mr Apostolakis and his instinct that the solicitor had withheld information from him rising to the surface once more.

He left the chair and crossed to the window, looking across to the hills before he turned to face her.

She seemed reluctant to answer his last question.

'Are you in some kind of trouble, Lexie?'

'No. I . . . ' Her voice trailed off, hesitant and unsure.

'But you're scared of . . . whom? Apostolakis? Someone else? And don't pretend you aren't scared of something,' he objected, forestalling her denial.

He leaned against the windowsill and folded his arms across his chest.

'I've seen it since you knew I'd been hired to find you.'

It was Lexie's turn to rise to her feet and pace restlessly around the small, cosy room. His gaze followed her wanderings, reading her anxiety and her indecision.

She glanced at him and then away, then went back to prod at the fire before she sat down again.

'Look, Mr Westwood . . . Steve,' she corrected, the sound of her voice and the brief smile that accompanied her alteration warming him inside. 'We all reach crossroads in our lives when we have to make choices. Sometimes we take the path of least resistance, sometimes we follow instinct and take a less travelled route. I made my decision. I can't do what other people want me to do. I can't sacrifice myself. Can you understand that?'

Steve nodded, a frown on his face as he absorbed her quiet but impassioned words.

'This has to do with your father's will and the search for you?'

'Yes.'

When she failed to elaborate, he straightened and went back to his armchair.

'If you want me to help you, you'll have to explain,' he said, resting his elbows on his knees as he held her gaze.

'I thought I had.'

'What about your grandfather?'

'What about him?' she shot back, concern lacing her voice once again.

'I was surprised to find you this far from Girvan, I thought — '

'You've found him, too?'

He was sorry he had upset her again but what was the big secret here? Why did she want to protect her grandfather, too?

'How does he feel about the will?' he asked.

'He is as determined as I am that I never comply with the conditions. There is no love lost between him and my father's side of the family . . . '

His gaze sharpened as Lexie broke off.

'Are you saying Alisdair Bennett is your mother's father?'

'Yes.'

'Then Bennett is not your true surname.'

'Yannis didn't tell you that?'

'No.' Another little cover up, Steve fumed. 'Then who are you?'

'Alexandra Olympios. Yannis is a cousin by marriage.'

Lexie felt tense as the silence dragged on. She linked her fingers tightly together and rested her hands in her lap, waiting for some response from the man who sat opposite her.

He looked angry. Very angry. She could well imagine that Yannis had spun him some false story.

The tick of the clock on the mantelpiece sounded unnaturally loud and vied only with the splutter of the fire.

Did Steve believe her? Had she told him enough for him to keep secret her whereabouts? She had said more than she should, but not as much as she could have done. That was to be resisted at all costs, as she doubted he would understand.

The truth, the absolute truth, sounded so far-fetched and archaic even to her, that she doubted she could convince him of the reality of the threat that hung over her.

She would give just a little more in the hope it would sway him.

'There are demands, instructions, in my father's will that I cannot comply with,' she explained now, choosing her words with care. 'My father's side of the family insisted I carry these out. I said no. There is a time limit and they are now more desperate to find me than ever. I don't want to be found.'

'This puts me in an awkward position,' Steve responded, a dark frown on his handsome face.

'I can see that.' Lexie held a breath. 'But I love my life here. I don't want to have to move again, to keep running. Please, Steve. Please don't tell Yannis where I am.'

6

Steve sat at his desk and stared sightlessly out of the window at the gathering dusk. He had been back in the office a day, and the discreet enquiries he had already made about Lexie's — Alexandra's — family, troubled him.

From what he had learned so far, her father, Dimitri, had been a ruthless dictator, ruling the family with an iron hand.

Judging by rumour of his treatment of two wives — Lexie's mother being the second — and a string of mistresses, he had no respect for women or their right to have a mind or a life of their own.

It was not hard to imagine him laying down the law to Lexie and trying to bind her to something against her will.

He couldn't imagine what it would

have been like for her to have that kind of upbringing and a father who showed only unreasonable discipline to all around him, including his daughter.

Even the wealth and luxury did nothing to soften the situation. And there was wealth there, almost beyond his imaginings.

Lexie's stand made sense to him now. He realised why she had chosen the life she had, free of those constraints.

She had cast off the outward, shallow trappings of money that had been a plague her whole life. His admiration for her inner strength and self-awareness increased.

He wanted to know more about the demands her father's will and her family were making on her, but he hadn't wanted to upset her further. As it was, she had been more relaxed by the time he left, that seductive smile and vibrant light back in her eyes.

Steve swallowed. The reluctance he had felt leaving her had both surprised and unsettled him. He didn't even know her, not really, and yet already she felt important to him.

There was an electrical tug he had been unable to ignore. And he didn't want to contemplate the very real possibility that he would never see her again.

Leaving the cottage had been difficult. He had been tempted to kiss her goodbye.

He had wanted to, just once, but he had known he couldn't. Instead, he had set a punishing pace back along the Southern Upland Way, one his old army sergeant would have been proud of, but nothing had displaced Lexie from his thoughts. He was behaving like the love-sick boy in the bar, Steve admitted.

Even the visit to his parents had been haunted by thoughts of her. Lexie Bennett had shot his commonsense to pieces.

Disgruntled by his thoughts, he was pondering what options he had with the report he must make to Yannis

Apostolakis, when Mike hobbled into the office.

'What are you doing here?' Steve complained, glancing at his watch.

Mike lowered himself into a chair.

'I've come in to pick up the information on the Piper job for my early appointment,' he informed, unperturbed by his partner's ill humour. He leaned his stick against Steve's desk. 'What's your excuse?'

'Just checking some information,' Steve hedged.

'To do with your Scottish trip?'

'Yeah.'

Mike's steady gaze focused on him. 'Problems?'

'Maybe.'

Several, Steve amended to himself, the primary one being a raven-haired beauty with smouldering dark eyes. He glanced up and saw Mike's eyes narrow a fraction.

'Anything I can help you with?' Mike asked.

'I'm just not happy with this case,'

Steve allowed after a short silence. 'Not happy at all.'

'What's wrong?'

'The client has been lying to me, and I don't feel that the motives for contacting Lexie Bennett are genuine.'

'But you did find her.'

'Yeah,' Steve confirmed with careful control. He'd found her all right. And look where it had got him. He cleared his throat and evaded his friend's questioning gaze. 'The facts don't check out.'

Mike raised an eyebrow, interest growing.

'Explain.'

'You don't have time for this,' Steve complained, not at all anxious to reveal his jumbled thoughts, much less his emotions, about the case. 'You have a family, remember?'

Without a word, Mike reached for the phone on the desk and dialled a number.

'Hi, Andrea,' he greeted, flashing Steve a grin. 'No, I'm still at the office. I have a couple of things to see to, but I won't be long.' He set down the receiver, leaned back in the chair and looked expectant. 'I'm all yours.'

Steve sighed in resignation and gave Mike an edited account of the events of the last few days. He included his concerns about Yannis Apostolakis and the information he had discovered about Lexie's real identity and the background on her father.

Mike gave a slow whistle as he digested the summing up.

'So what are you thinking?' he asked.

'That I shouldn't divulge her whereabouts,' Steve replied. 'She isn't a runaway teenager, Mike. Hasn't she the right to make her own decisions and guard her privacy if that's what she wants?'

'Yes, of course. But?' he pressed, correctly discerning an underlying hesitation.

Steve sighed and dropped his feet back to the floor.

'But we were hired to do a job, and

I went beyond the brief by talking to her. On the other hand, the client lied. I think there is more going on here than meets the eye.'

'I agree.' Mike nodded. 'What is it that's worrying you specifically?' he queried with a small frown.

'It didn't take me long to find her. They can hire someone else to do the same, someone who won't hesitate to give them what they want,' Steve opined, voicing the point Lexie had made to him just before he had left.

'That isn't your responsibility.'

Steve averted his gaze, unwilling to explain just how much he suddenly viewed Lexie and her well-being as his concern. He crossed his arms and leaned on the desk, trying to think through his point of view.

'Look, I have to go back to the client. What am I going to do? Lie? I don't like doing that, not for me and not for the reputation of the agency.'

'There may be a small snag,' Mike ventured, looking uncomfortable.

'And that is?'

'Don't blow a gasket, OK? Mr Apostolakis rang a couple of times while you were gone and Joyce finally put him on to me.'

Steve groaned under the weight of premonition.

'Mike — '

'I'm sorry, but I told him you were in Scotland, that you had a lead on her grandfather in Girvan.'

'Damn it, Mike! I thought we had a rule in this agency that we don't give out information on the phone . . . even our juniors know that,' Steve groused.

He cursed for a moment and ran a hand through his hair in exasperation.

'Now what do I tell him?'

'You know I'll back you whatever you decide. I'm sorry about it, but none of us realised it wasn't a straightforward job,' Mike apologised again. 'Waive the fee. Tell him the trail went cold.'

Steve rubbed his hands over his face.

'So I just leave it open? What if he

hires someone else and does discover where she is?' he persisted, realising too late he had roused more speculation.

'Why are you so interested in this woman?'

'I'm not.'

'Sure!' Mike's smile became teasing. 'Has she fallen for the Westwood charm?'

'Drop it, Mike.'

Steve scowled at his friend, not sharing his amusement.

'Can we get back to the problem?'

'Which is the case . . . or the girl? What's she like, anyway?'

'How should I know?' Steve snapped, his patience wearing thin. 'I barely saw her, let alone get to know her in any way.'

Mike laughed aloud as he reached out for his stick and levered himself to his feet.

'You're right, partner.' He smiled slyly. 'You'd better not lie to the client. You're far too transparent.'

Steve bit back a heated, impolite

retort, and watched in silence as Mike collected a file, waved a cheery good-night, and left the office.

* * *

Alone once more, his temper continued to simmer. He felt his conversation with Mike had taken him two steps back, and he still had to decide the nature of his report to Mr Apostolakis. It was nothing at all to do with Lexie personally, he assured himself again and again. It was a matter of principle of conscience. He did not appreciate being lied to by anyone, and he loathed injustices and people who hurt others for their own ends.

The concern that someone else would be hired to track down Lexie, someone with less qualms than he had about handing her over, was a real one. He just couldn't let that happen . . . couldn't walk away and leave Lexie to her fate.

It was none of his business and he

didn't even know what threat she had hanging over her, but he did know she was scared and that her family were ruthless in obtaining their own ends.

She was a sparky lady, but he doubted she could withstand the might of a determined bunch of uncles and cousins for long. And if they did find her, who knew what they would do? He couldn't divulge to Mr Apostolakis what he knew about Lexie, nor could he vent his anger at being lied to in the first place. That would only confirm he had found her. For her sake, he had to tread carefully.

He swore aloud in frustration. He was angry with Mike for having his accident and passing the job on to him, angry with Yannis Apostolakis for just about everything, angry with Lexie for getting under his skin. But mostly, he was angry with himself for allowing the combination of all the above to unsettle him.

Damn Lexie. If only he could get her out of his mind. He thought about her all the time. Her mass of black hair, her kind, laughing eyes the colour of rich chocolate, that warm smile that made him want to kiss her . . . only she hadn't been smiling when she had thought of her family finding her.

He must decide what he was to do and he didn't have that much time . . .

★ ★ ★

'Are you sickening for something, lassie?'

Lexie glanced up from her final task in closing up the bar for the night and looked across at Ross.

'No, I'm fine. Why?'

'You've lost some of your sparkle,' her employer commented. 'You're sure you're all right?'

'Positive.'

She managed a bright smile and after saying good-night to Ross and her workmates, she pedalled swiftly home.

Once there, she double checked all

the locks and windows then went to the kitchen to fix herself a milky drink. For the first time since she had moved here, she felt anxious being alone and isolated.

It was Steve's success in finding her that had robbed her of her illusion of safety. And since his departure, she had been acutely nervous, watchful and wary of strangers who came into the bar. She felt as if she was living dangerously close to the edge.

She had intended discussing the latest developments with her grandfather but before she had the opportunity, he had called the bar to cancel their weekly get-together as he had developed a nasty bout of bronchitis.

He had sounded so awful, but he had been adamant that she was not to visit the house, that he had people to watch out for him. With reluctance, she had agreed. She hadn't wanted to add to his worries. Telling him about Steve would have to wait until he was well.

Steve . . . Lexie poured her drink

and went to sit by the fire. She had thought about him far too much since she had watched him walk away from the cottage and out of her life almost a week ago.

There had been no word from him but he had promised to respect her wishes. A smile curved her mouth as she thought of his last words that afternoon.

'But what about your report to Yannis?' she had asked with concern.

He had smiled that heart-melting smile that made her warm just to think of it.

'You leave him to me. I told him I would find you, not that I would say where you were.'

Lexie curled up in the chair and cradled her mug in her hands. She would love to be a fly on the wall when Steve told Yannis he couldn't help locate her. Her smile faded. If Steve did tell him. A ripple of concern ran through her. There was no option but to trust him.

This new attempt to find her, the pressure her family exerted on her and their desperate determination to bring her to heel like some obedient lap dog, roused her indignation. She would not be made to feel guilty for choosing a life that was different from the one her father had mapped out for her. She would not allow them to force her to do something against her will.

When she had first hatched her plan to disappear, it had all seemed overly elaborate and dramatic. Giving up her friends had been difficult, and it still pained her that she could only see and talk to Jillian in cautious and roundabout ways. And Gramps . . . she wanted to be free to see him, be with him and take care of him, not stuck here, afraid to venture out in case Yannis had more people searching for her.

This was all down to her father's arrogance and control. He had never cared about her, never shown her an iota of affection or understanding, blaming everyone for the fact he never had a son to carry on his empire. She was expendable, just like her mother . . . a tool to bring him what he wanted. His dominance would not rule her from his grave.

Lexie went up to bed, but once there, she found she was too restless to sleep and unable to push her worries from her mind. Provided she could evade Yannis, she would be all right for the future.

There had been some money even her father could not touch and she had been able to secrete some savings for a rainy day. If she was careful and kept her wages coming in, she would manage just fine.

It was not the sort of lifestyle she had known for the first eighteen years of her life. Far from it. But she had never been interested in luxuries or her father's appetite for extravagances.

She thought now of the wardrobes that were full of the designer clothes she had left behind the last time she had closed the door on her father's opulent London penthouse, and the jewels.

None of that mattered to her, nor the private jet, the palatial yacht, the Italian sports cars.

Yes, it had been easy to walk away without a backward glance. Nothing would induce her to return.

7

'How do you expect me to type letters for you when you present me with notes written in this meaningless scrawl?'

Steve glanced up from the file on his desk as Joyce's complaint, delivered in the most sarcastic and cutting tones of her vast repertoire, invaded his concentration.

His gaze clashed with her implacable blue one. As Mike smothered a smirk at the nearby desk, Steve shot him a violent glare.

'I'm sorry,' he said as Joyce dropped some papers on his desk. 'I'll check them over.'

'Thank you. Now, did you take some money from the petty cash tin?'

Steve raised his chin, feeling as defiant as an errant schoolboy called before the formidable headmistress.

'Yes. I had to send a package to a

client and I didn't have enough cash on me.'

'I see.'

Joyce sighed with resigned martyrdom.

'I suppose it is pointless to ask if you got a receipt?' she added.

'I forgot.'

'What a surprise,' she offered as a parting shot before she smiled at Mike and left the office.

'At least there's one woman who is immune to your masculine charm,' Mike teased, knowing full well Steve had pressed for Joyce's appointment for precisely that reason.

'Just because you have her wrapped round your little finger,' Steve complained, grumpily.

He'd faced down roaring drill sergeants, surely he could cope with one crotchety secretary.

Joyce was severe and had disapproved of him from day one. But she was efficient, loyal and discreet, and as far as he was concerned, her most appealing feature was her more mature years and a complete disinterest in him on a personal level.

Their last secretary had pursued him with overpowering vigour. Mike was unfailingly amused, but Steve was tired of women setting their caps at him, tired of drawing interested glances. He wasn't the Casanova Mike teased him to be. He wanted a family one day, wanted to settle down.

There had been women, several of them, just no-one who had that something special that had made him want to stick around.

He had joined the army straight out of school and then there had been the business venture with Mike. It had been hard work getting established and securing a future. He had neither the time nor the inclination for a meaningful relationship. Besides, he hadn't found the right woman yet.

The sudden vision of Lexie filled his mind. In the last week, he had determined he would get her out of his system, but he hadn't succeeded yet. At least a dozen times an hour thoughts of her disturbed his concentration.

Now it was over. He had made his report to Yannis Apostolakis, had explained that the information he'd been given had been insufficient and there was nothing more he could do to help.

The Greek's smooth acceptance of the apparent failure of the mission still left a bad taste in his mouth.

It was all too neat, had been tied up too easily. He wished he knew what the solicitor was up to.

Forget it, he told himself for the hundredth time with a burst of inner anger. He was losing his objectivity and he had no more time to waste on what was past. Once and for all, he would put Lexie out of his mind.

* * *

'What do you mean, he isn't there?'

Lexie clutched the information given to her in a broad Scots accent. Alarm sent shivers down her spine.

She had been phoning her grandfather every day, and then this afternoon there had been no reply.

Concerned he had taken a turn for the worse, she had contacted his neighbour, a level-headed widow who was a retired nurse. She had gone to check on him and then called Lexie back.

'I can't understand it, Lexie. I saw him yesterday evening and he was resting comfortably — told me not to fuss, if you please. I've checked all over. His bed hasn't been slept in.'

'But that's ridiculous,' Lexie exclaimed, her anxiety growing. 'The doctor told him to rest.'

'I know. There's no sense in it.'

Lexie tried to control her fears and maintain her calm.

'And there's no note? Nothing at all?'

'I'm sorry.'

When she hung up, with the neighbour promising to call if she had any news,

Lexie went to the staff room to take her break. She was unable to comprehend what had happened.

There was no way Gramps would have gone off without telling her, she was positive about that. Only yesterday, he had said how low he still felt and how much he was looking forward to the peace of relaxing at home.

She returned to the telephone and put a call through to his doctor.

He assured her there had been no question of a turn for the worse and that her grandfather had not been hospitalised. Indeed, he could not explain her grandfather's absence either.

So where was he? Why had he gone off without a word to anyone? Lexie chewed her lip and walked back to the staff room once more. If she could just make sense of this.

She hesitated. No. She couldn't consider the possibility that Yannis or one of the family had found him.

She was not usually indecisive or

104

given to panic, but she felt at a loss to know what to do. Whom could she approach for advice? Only Gramps and Jillian knew the situation anyway.

She swallowed as a thought crossed her mind. There was one other person who knew — Steve Westwood. Had he broken his promise? Had he led Yannis to her grandfather?

With a frown, she searched in her handbag for the card Steve had given her. For several moments she stared at it. She had to know one way or the other. And if he hadn't told Yannis, he was the only person she knew who would know what to do.

She was scared now, really scared. If Yannis had her grandfather, if he was used as bait to make her do what they wanted, how would she be able to fight them?

Ultimately, they would coerce her — by force if they had to. They were that desperate, that greedy.

Had this last year all been for nothing? If something happened to

Gramps, she would never forgive herself. Why had she even imagined she could ever outsmart Yannis and the others? They had too much to lose to ever let her go.

Tears pricked her eyes as she looked down at the business card she held in her hands. It seemed so dramatic to even think this was necessary. Then she thought of her grandfather and all she had to lose . . .

It had been a frustrating day, Steve mused, as he put the finishing touches to a security proposal and snapped the file closed. He had no evening engagement and he was looking forward to going home, the pub, anywhere that would take his mind off her.

Lexie . . . she invaded his thoughts like a demon, refusing all his efforts to be free of her.

The intercom buzzed on his desk and he stabbed at the button angrily.

'Yes?' he snapped.

Joyce's voice rang with aggrieved dignity.

'There is a Miss Bennett on the line for you.'

Steve sucked in a breath and cast a hasty glance at Mike, hoping his friend had not heard. But a grin and the raising of eyebrows told him otherwise. Concentrating on the call, he spoke to Joyce again.

'Put her through, please, Joyce.'

There was a momentary pause during which he experienced an alarming impatience and eagerness to just hear her voice. And then it came, tentative and unsure.

'Hello?'

'Lexie! I didn't expect — '

'Did you say something to Yannis?' she demanded, cutting across his opening words. 'You promised — '

'Just hold on a minute,' he broke in, forming an interruption of his own, her heated questioning dampening his initial pleasure at hearing from her. 'I didn't tell him anything, Lexie, only that I couldn't help him. Now take a breath and tell me what's wrong.'

There was a moment of silence during which Steve cast another glance at his partner to find Mike watching and listening with evident interest.

He smothered a sigh and tried to ignore the way just talking with her still knotted him up inside.

'Lexie?' he pressed as the silence continued.

'How much?'

The softness of the delivery betrayed a waver in her voice.

'How much what?' he asked with sudden wariness.

'Would it cost to . . . ' She paused and stumbled over the next words. 'To hire you.'

Steve sat up straighter in his chair, all his senses instantly at attention as he recognised a thread of fear in her voice.

'Lexie, what is it? What is it? What's happened?'

'It's my grandfather. He's gone missing. What if Yannis has found him? Steve, I don't know what to do.'

'All right, let's start at the beginning. I want you to tell me what you know, why you think your grandfather has disappeared,' he told her gently. 'Take your time.'

He listened, his concern increasing as Lexie explained the events of the last few days.

It certainly sounded odd, and given what he knew of the circumstances, he had to agree with her. He just couldn't see any way that her grandfather would take off — ill or otherwise — without contacting her. Something must have happened.

But — he didn't even want to consider that Yannis might have something to do with it.

'What if they try to use my grandfather to make me do what they want?' she finished, her voice trembling.

'Lexie, what's in the will? What are they trying to make you do?'

A silence followed his question, a silence that lengthened until he thought he would snap with the tension.

He heard her uneven breathing. He couldn't bear it if she cried.

'I can't,' she finally whispered. 'Steve, I can't do it, I don't want to do it, but, Gramps . . . My father, he . . . '

Steve swallowed a sudden lump in his throat at her barely suppressed emotion. He met Mike's sombre gaze.

'What about your father, Lexie?' he queried quietly.

'The will. I should have known I couldn't fight them. I'll do whatever it takes to protect Gramps.'

'No.'

Anger curled inside him at whatever it was that frightened her so much. He tried to calm down and moderate his tone.

'It's OK, Lexie, you don't have to tell me. Just listen. Until we know for certain that Yannis has anything to do with this, you are not to do anything foolish, least of all contact him or your family. You must promise that you will do nothing in the meantime.'

'But I have to go to Girvan. I

could check the house, see what I can find out.'

'Absolutely not.'

'But — '

'But nothing.'

Steve pulled a pad and pen towards him.

'Lexie, I'm going to help you, but you have to trust me and you have to do what I say. Do you understand?'

There was another pause, and he held his breath until he heard her soft answer.

'Yes.'

'All right then. Where are you phoning from?'

'The pub.'

'Give me the number there.'

He jotted it down and tapped his pen on the desktop as he did a quick think.

'OK. Can you stay at the pub tonight, or with someone else? Think, Lexie. Is there anyone who could help you out?'

'I don't want to involve other people in this.'

Steve ignored her stubborn resistance.

'And I don't want you out at that cottage on your own. I'm serious, Lexie. You are not to rush off anywhere by yourself until we find out what's happening,' he insisted.

'Steve . . . '

'Stay out of trouble. Promise me.'

He heard a deep sigh.

'All right. I promise.'

'Just wait for me, Lexie. I'll be there as soon as I can.'

He hated to hang up the phone and break the contact with her. She was alone with her worries and troubles with no-one to turn to. At least she had called him and hadn't rushed off on her own, possibly into a trap.

'You're going back to Scotland.'

Mike's statement drew Steve from his reverie and he pulled himself together to give his partner a concise brief on the details of Lexie's call.

'So I've got to go. I can't possibly leave her there alone,' he finished.

'What do you want me to do

from here?' Mike asked sombrely, his humour at Steve's reaction to Lexie long since gone.

For several minutes, they thrashed out the problem and agreed on a plan of action. But Steve was reluctant to force the issue or show themselves to Yannis until he reached Scotland and had assessed the situation.

'There is still the possibility that there could be a simple and innocent explanation to this,' he ventured.

'But you doubt it.'

'Yeah. Lexie's intelligent and doesn't seem the panicky type.'

He leaned back in his chair, a dark frown on his face.

'Whatever it is they have hanging over her from this will, it really frightens her, Mike.'

Mike watched him, his gaze speculative.

'This isn't your fault.'

'But it was me who led them there.'

'It sounded a perfectly straightforward job,' Mike replied.

He sighed and shook his head.

'Look, if it wasn't you, it would have been someone else.'

'That makes me feel a whole lot better,' Steve said angrily.

His friend ignored the sarcasm.

'Then blame me. I told Apostolakis you were in Girvan.'

'You weren't to know.'

'Exactly. And neither were you.'

Mike linked his hands behind his head and smiled slightly.

'So, now you feel you owe Lexie . . . or is it something else?'

That wasn't what he was feeling about Lexie at all, not by a long way. But he wasn't about to tell Mike how complicated his emotions were, how involved he was becoming.

For now, he had to collate what he would need for the trip, pack a bag at his flat and pick up his motorbike.

There was no way he was going to get the overnight train and then mess about hiring another car. He'd be halfway there before the train left Euston and if he was lucky, he'd have time to check out Alisdair Bennett's place in Girvan before he met Lexie at the pub in the morning.

He just hoped she would do what he'd told her. He didn't want to examine the fear that knotted his insides at the thought of something happening to her. From what he'd discovered about her family, they seemed ruthless enough to force her into doing whatever it was they wanted.

But he wouldn't let that happen. He would do whatever was necessary to protect her.

8

It had been a long, lonely night. Lexie hadn't known what excuse to give Ross and his wife, Isabel, for wanting to stay at the pub and in the end, she had said she needed to be near the telephone in case her grandfather called. At least it had basis in fact.

There was no telephone at her cottage, and she couldn't be more worried, more desperate to hear some good news. This morning she was tense, her underlying fear for her grandfather increasing.

It had been nearly twenty-four hours now since she had tried to reach him and probably more since he had left his house, voluntarily or not.

The night had been sleepless, each minute dragging into the next. She had tossed and turned in the strange bed, the occasional rumble of a car along the road bringing her to anxious attention.

Finally morning had come, but it had brought no pleasure in a new day, only the continual weight of worry.

Now, as she helped Ross and Isabel prepare the pub for business, she was subdued.

Half an hour before they were due to open, she was polishing the horse brasses that hung on the upright beams, when there was a loud knocking at the outer door. She froze and shivered as her imagination ran riot. Had the family found her?

She swung her startled gaze to Ross. Both he and Isabel had been kind and patient but she knew they were puzzled at her strange behaviour. Seeing her rooted to the spot, Ross set down the laden tray he was carrying, shot her a questioning glance, then went to answer the door.

Lexie sucked in several steadying breaths and told herself she was being ridiculous. Lack of sleep and worry about Gramps was making her paranoid. It could be any one of a number of people at the door, for any one of a number of perfectly ordinary reasons.

Calming her nerves, she turned back to continue her task.

'It's someone for you, Lexie,' Ross called in his deep Scots burr.

For the second time Lexie hesitated, her cloth suspended in mid polish. Her heart began to hammer beneath her ribs. Slowly, she turned round.

'Steve!'

Relief washed through her as she stared at him. She had hardly allowed herself to believe he would come all the way back to Scotland.

It had been enough that he listened, gave her strength, would know what to do. That he was here already was more than she could ever have expected. Just looking at him brought a thrill and a fire to her blood.

Dressed in jeans and a dark brown leather jacket, he held a motorcycle helmet in one gloved hand. He looked dead tired, and she realised he must have been on the road for hours. His jaw was stubbled, his hair tousled, those smoky grey eyes betraying his weariness.

Before she could gather her wits, he closed the distance between them. He stopped in front of her, so close she could feel his warmth, her senses teased by his subtle male scent. She looked up at him, uncaring that her gratitude at seeing him and her fear for her grandfather were reflected in her over-bright eyes.

'You came,' she murmured unnecessarily, barely aware that Ross and Isabel stood nearby and watched them curiously.

'Of course. Didn't I say I would?'

He pulled off a glove, reached out a hand and cupped her cheek. His grey gaze scanned her pale face and the shadows beneath her eyes with concern.

'You OK?'

Lexie nodded, unable to trust her voice.

Faced with his kindness, she felt something inside her want to give in and release the pent-up emotions that had kept her on a knife-edge of anxiety for the last hours. She bit her lip. She never cried, and she was not about to start now. Her gaze locked with his as she battled against the sudden threat of tears.

He closed his eyes briefly, the absent brush of his thumb along her cheekbone making her shiver then he took another step up to her and held her against him.

For a moment she allowed herself the luxury of resting her face against his chest, absorbing the comfort, drawing his strength. He just rested his chin on top of her head and waited, giving her time.

'Is there somewhere we can talk?'

Steve's voice, warm and low, finally refocused her wavering attention. Disconcerted, she stepped back, breaking the unsettling contact of his hand on her face.

She felt confused and slightly embarrassed. All the awareness she had experienced the last time she had seen this man was still there — only now, it was stronger than ever.

'Of course,' she replied in belated response to his query, then she cast a hasty glance at Ross and Isabel. 'Could I have a few minutes, please?'

'No problem, lassie.'

Ross smiled, collecting the tray he had abandoned when he went to the door.

'Take whatever time you need.'

Lexie led Steve through to the staff rest room, glad to find that it was empty. No doubt the rest of the bar and kitchen staff were already hard at work. She turned and watched as Steve set his helmet on the table, removed his other glove, then shrugged out of his leather jacket.

For a moment she allowed her gaze to linger on him. He was so attractive, casual and yet exciting, even in simple jeans and thick jumper.

As he ran a hand tiredly over his eyes, she felt guilty that she had put him to so much trouble and taken up his valuable time.

'When did you last eat or sleep?' she asked, her voice laced with concern.

He sent her a small smile and shrugged, as if it was of no importance.

'A long time ago.'

'Sit down, please, and I'll put on some coffee. Will toast be all right, or can I get you something more substantial from the kitchen?'

'Toast will be fine.'

She felt his gaze on her as she prepared the refreshments at the small counter set aside for the staffs' breaks. A tingle ran up her spine, prickling at the back of her neck, and she ignored the sudden impulse to rub at it, as if by doing so she could erase his effect on her.

Taking off her pinny, she folded it and set it on the counter, then put a plate of toast, some butter and homemade jam, and two mugs of fresh coffee on the table.

She sat opposite Steve, nervous, alarmed at how acutely conscious she was of his presence, his every small move and shift of expression.

She knew that if anyone could help her find her grandfather it was him, and yet instinctively, she was aware that spending any time at all with him was not going to be easy. The way she felt with him and her reaction to him was hard to ignore.

★ ★ ★

Steve drank his coffee and watched her through hooded eyes. She wore no make-up, looked scared, and obviously hadn't slept at all, and yet she was still beautiful and irresistible.

He hadn't meant to touch her, he just hadn't been able to help it when she had looked so lost and alone. Her skin had been baby-soft, the touch of

123

her hair like silk on his face.

Her dark eyes looked haunted now. He could see she was worried sick about her grandfather, and his own concern had increased since his arrival in Scotland in the early hours.

He didn't want to tell her about that — not yet. More than anything, he wanted to make her smile, just once.

'I'm glad to say you make better coffee than Mrs Peterson.'

For a moment she looked perplexed, then realisation dawned that he would have been to see her old landlady in his search for her.

A hint of amusement vied with the clouds that shadowed her eyes. And then she smiled. It was a teasing, mischievous smile that momentarily made him silently catch his breath.

Steve dragged his gaze away, unprepared for the intensity of his reaction to her. He helped himself to toast, forcing himself to concentrate on the normality of his actions as he lightly buttered it and added a spoonful of fruity jam.

While he had his unexpected breakfast, he kept things light between them, talking about Mrs Peterson and then about his journey up.

He had done the trip from London in record time, his powerful bike eating up the miles. Thankfully he had not attracted the unwanted attentions of the motorway police.

He cradled his half-empty mug in his hands, his mood serious once more. It was his early morning excursion to Girvan that was on his mind now. Glancing up, he met the half-fearful, half-hopeful expression in Lexie's eyes and knew he couldn't keep it from her any longer.

'I went to your grandfather's house,' he began, noticing the way her fingers tightened their grip on her mug.

'And?'

The whisper barely carried across the gap between them.

'There was definitely someone watching the house, Lexie. I was careful not to be seen and I double checked. There was no doubt,' he said, trying to keep his voice calm and professional.

'I see. Then it's true. Yannis must have found him.'

The flat defeat in her voice tore at his heart. He swallowed as he watched the light dim from her eyes.

'It looks that way. You can't think of anywhere else at all that he could have gone?'

'No. I've racked my brains, but there is nothing I can think of to explain why he's gone, why he hasn't called me. Only Yannis and the family.'

She looked at him, her eyes wide and anxious.

'Why haven't they contacted me if they have him?'

'He probably hasn't told them where you are. They'll be relying on him for information.'

'But he's ill. What if . . . '

Steve reached out to cover her hand with his and found it cold and trembling.

'Lexie, it's in their own interests that

he's well. He'd be no use to them otherwise,' he attempted to reassure her, hoping it was true. 'And he wouldn't risk trying to contact you himself if he was with them.'

'So what do we do?'

'We wait.'

He saw the doubt and resistance on her face and pre-empted her interruption.

'I know it's hard and I can only imagine what you must be feeling. But for the time being, this is our best option, please believe me.'

'But — '

'Lexie, listen, I know what I'm doing. My partner, Mike, is organising someone to keep a watch on Yannis to see if we get a lead on your grandfather. We should have some news from there later. We can't rush into this without some idea what is going on and without a proper plan.'

What Steve said made sense. Lexie sighed with a mixture of frustration and resignation. She hated the waiting, the feeling of being so helpless and ineffectual.

'I know you're right,' she allowed with an apologetic smile, withdrawing her hand from the disturbing contact with his. 'Thank you for helping me.'

'That's OK.'

Their gazes locked for a moment, then he straightened; suddenly business-like.

'What time do you finish work here today?'

'Three o'clock.'

She felt disappointed when he stood up from the table. She wasn't quite ready to see him go, to lose his strength and support.

'I have a few things to take care of,' he told her as he pulled on his leather jacket and picked up his helmet and gloves. 'I'll be back by three to take you home and we'll talk some more.'

'OK.'

He walked around the table as she stood up, his grey eyes warm and understanding.

There was a brief flash of something else, something deeper and elusive that was gone before she recognised it.

'Everything will be all right, Lexie,' he promised her, his voice low and sure, sending a glow of awareness through her.

He hesitated for a moment then dropped a light kiss on her forehead.

'I'll see you later.'

* * *

Lexie was glad she was kept busy, that the hectic activity in the bar and kitchen for the next few hours allowed scant time for her mind to linger on both her grandfather and Steve.

It felt good him being here . . . too good. She was unused to relying on anyone else for anything, but most worrying to her peace of mind was how long she could deny to herself how attracted she was to him.

It was more than his kindness, his support and help in trying to locate her grandfather, more than his outward looks. The first time she had seen him, she had been aware of something stronger, something elemental that touched a part deep inside her.

True to his word, Steve returned to the bar in time for a late sandwich lunch. He had changed, shaved, and looked less tired and crumpled round the edges than when he had left her, and she was surprised to discover he had rented the other half of the cottages from her landlord.

For the next couple of days, or however long it took, they would be neighbours.

Her colleagues were curious as Steve waited around until she was ready to leave.

She had told Ross and Isabel that she had a few family problems, and hoped that would halt any unwanted, if well-meaning, questions she did not know how to answer.

They walked back to her cottage together, wheeling her bicycle. She didn't know if it was a good omen or not, but Steve had brought sunshine and warmth with him. Daffodils glowed in the gardens and along the roadside near the village, the hills shone, fresh and clear, and the glen seemed to bask in the full flush of spring.

Beside the lane, the burn gurgled on its way to the nearby river. As they neared the cottage, they disturbed a dipper. It rose from its underwater search for larvae and insects and hesitated a moment, bobbing on a half-submerged rock.

'Are you working this evening?' Steve asked when she unlocked the door and led the way inside the cottage.

'No. I have some time owing for the extra shifts I did when others were away with the flu.'

She walked across and cleared the remains of the fire that had burned itself out in the grate the day before, then set about laying a new one.

'I spoke to Mike,' Steve told her, handing her a couple of logs to put on top of the kindling. 'He has no definite news yet but I'll call him again tomorrow.'

Her heart sank, even though she knew it was unrealistic to expect immediate results. She just had so much riding on the outcome.

That the family would use her grandfather to make her do what they wanted was too awful to bear.

'Steve, we have to find him. I dread to think what will happen if we don't. I've fought against this for so long but I won't let anything happen to Gramps. I'll do whatever it takes.'

'Lexie, tell me what it is.' His voice was gentle but insistent as he picked up her tremor and her fear. 'I'm going to do all I can to help you, but I need to understand. What else is going on here?'

Slowly, she rose to her feet and faced him. His gaze was steady, determined, and she sighed as she recognised that he was not going to let her back off from him. Not this time.

She needed his help. She had to trust him. However much she had hoped to avoid it, there was really no choice but to tell him the whole, sordid tale.

9

By the time Lexie had made some tea and she and Steve were sitting by the fire, she had managed to work herself into a bit of a panic. Now the moment had arrived, she had no idea where to begin. Her background had always been a source of embarrassment, and she made a point never to discuss her past.

She didn't want it known the kind of life she had led. Indeed, only Jillian knew the true identity and ways of her family. From the age of eighteen, she had used her mother's maiden name and distanced herself in every way possible from all that had been before.

Aware of Steve's gaze on her, she looked up and saw the speculation in the ash-grey eyes. She could not stall any longer.

'I don't know if you've heard anything about my father.'

'Not much,' he allowed, crossing his legs. 'I'd rather hear from you.'

'I suppose it would help you to understand the current situation if I gave you some background on the kind of man my father was.'

She paused for a moment and took a sip of her tea, her fingers tightening on the mug.

'His first wife brought my father a couple of new businesses as a dowry. It was an arranged marriage. A means to an end as far as my father was concerned. She failed to produce children — he was bent on an heir for his empire — so she was discarded as worthless. He had the companies, after all, and she had become a liability.

'It was unfortunate for my mother that she was caught when my father cast his net once more. She was a beautiful woman, inheriting my grandfather's Scottish gentleness and my grandmother's English diffidence.

Flattered by the attentions of a charming, wealthy Greek magnate almost twice her age, who showered her with gifts and all the fine things in life, she was swept off her feet and married before the year was out.

'But my father's charm was surface deep. He didn't care about my mother, only saw her as a healthy, biddable, young woman, a good investment in terms of providing him with a son. She failed, too, because after giving birth to me, a girl of all things, much to my father's disbelief, she had two miscarriages and couldn't have any more children.

'My father didn't believe any woman was worth much beyond looking decorative and producing sons. Cowed by his cruel and domineering ways, my mother, with whom he was getting more angry, never recovered her sense of self, her worth, and she died a broken woman when I was ten.'

Lexie darted a look at Steve and saw the brooding expression on his face. There was an anger that had begun to fire in his grey eyes. She sat back in the chair, took a deep breath, and went on with the sordid family history.

'Of course, I didn't understand all the details of all this at the time,' she elaborated, trying to stay calm in the rush of emotion that always threatened when she thought of her mother's unhappiness. 'The only thing my mother braved my father's wrath for was me.'

Steve sat forward and set his mug aside. He looked as if he wanted to say something, but Lexie held up a hand, knowing if she didn't get this all out now, she never would.

'After she died, I was bundled off to boarding school — out of sight, out of mind. But I loved it there. Anything was better than a loveless, motherless home or being sent to family in Greece. There were holidays to be endured, of course, but there was the sanctuary of the school until I was eighteen.'

'And then?' Steve prompted as she hesitated.

'Then things really began to get interesting.'

She gave a humourless laugh and leaned forward to throw another log on the fire. For a moment, she stared into the dancing flames.

'A string of beautiful women decorated my father's arm, but there were to be no more children. He was an angry, disappointed man with no son to groom to continue the dynasty he founded. So he selected the brightest and most ruthless, young man from the family, a second cousin of mine, to be his protégé and heir. Costa would be schooled and moulded, and eventually would assume control after my father's death. By uniting the family and their business interests, my uncles and cousins would increase their holdings and their millions.'

She rose to her feet, unable to look at him as she imparted the most humiliating piece of information. With

138

her back to him, she crossed to the window and looked out as dusk began to shadow the contours of the hills.

'Lexie?'

'Costa is two years older than me, and so spiteful. He was a cruel, nasty, little boy, grown into an evil man. I hated holidays when we were thrown together. He was a bully, even then, and I suffered at his hands, but he never broke my spirit. But then my father . . . '

Her words trailed off. She couldn't tell him this. It sounded so absurd, like something out of the dark ages. She did not think he would ever understand. No one outside her family could appreciate living under her father's rule, his lack of consideration, his manipulation of people.

'What is it, Lexie? What did your father do?'

Steve's soft enquiry drew her from her thoughts. Her hands clutched the edge of the windowsill and she kept her gaze averted.

'He made an arrangement with Costa.'

There was a pause, and she held her breath as she waited for Steve's response.

'What kind of an arrangement?'

'I was eighteen when I discovered what my father had done. He confiscated my passport, allowed me a semblance of independence while at the same time he had me watched. He thought my show of defiance was just that, a show, that I would never dare to truly go against him. His law was absolute and he never doubted his power. That was his big mistake.

'I never ceased to be a disappointment to my father who thought women should be leggy and reed-thin and the fewer the brains and displays of self-will the better. I had too many curves and far too much of a mind of my own, and you can imagine his distaste when the ugly duckling grew into an ugly duck and not the proverbial swan.'

'That's rubbish, Lexie — '

140

'I wanted a life of my own.' She interrupted his gallant rebuttal of her father's assessment of her. 'My father saw a way of off-loading me and turning it to his advantage. But fortunately for me, he was an arrogant man. He thought he could control everything, run everything to his own timetable, even his own death.'

She sighed, drew the curtains, and paced about the room.

'Costa's little deal with my father backfired on him because my father found a way to display a final act of power and control over me and the rest of the family. His pièce de resistance. Costa wanted me, the one woman who had never cowed to him, but my father ensured he wouldn't get me for nothing.

'In order for my uncles, cousins and Costa to get their hands on my father's personal fortune as well as his business, I have to marry Costa within eighteen months of my father's death.'

'That is completely outrageous!'

Anger drove Steve from his chair after a moment of stunned disbelief following Lexie's bombshell. He thought of the kind of life she must have had, of the tyrant her father had been and her obvious fear of Costa. He ignored the flash of personal interest that threatened his objectivity.

He had to push aside just how disturbing it was to imagine her marrying anyone, let alone the appalling Costa. He blocked out thoughts of her being terrorised by him in her youth and worse than that, what her life would be like with him now. He crossed the room and turned her to face him, dismayed at her pallor, the dullness of her eyes.

'It isn't going to happen, Lexie.'

'You don't understand what they are capable of when something means this much to them.'

'Didn't you try to contest the will?'

Reluctantly he let her go when she shrugged away from him and wrapped her arms around herself. He hated the protective gesture, hated that he was so angry on her behalf that his question had sounded brusque, challenging.

She didn't need this from him. All he wanted at that moment was to wrap his own arms around her, keep her safe, never let her go. Instead he watched impotently as she went back to her chair by the fire.

'My father was buried in Greece, in the family plot on his private island, and I didn't even go to his funeral. Don't you think that's terrible?' she asked, almost as if she was talking to herself, examining her feelings of guilt.

Steve felt her pain and wanted more than anything to make it go away.

'No, it's not terrible, Lexie.'

'He'd taken away my passport. Of course, I could have applied for a replacement, but I couldn't have gone to their territory. They would have found a way to keep me there and married me off to Costa against my will, anything to get their hands on the money.'

'They sound a delightful bunch,' Steve glowered, anger building up inside him.

'The collective force of uncles and cousins, all greedy for a share of my father's private fortune is a sight to behold,' she agreed with disgust. 'I've seen them in action. I had no idea what to do, no-one but my grandfather to turn to.'

'So you went into hiding.'

'I thought that once the deadline passed it would all be over.'

Her hands shook as she brushed back the fall of her lustrous hair.

'I should have known they would fight any way they could to bring me to heel. Now, my grandfather — just to think of Costa fills me with revulsion.'

Steve swallowed at the fear on her face. She looked so lost . . . scared and vulnerable. He went across and squatted down in front of her, taking her hands in his.

'Costa won't do anything to you again, Lexie, I promise.'

'They already have more money than they know what to do with, and they have the companies. Steve, I can't sacrifice myself so they can line their bottomless bank accounts.'

'You won't have to.'

He tilted up her chin and saw the gleam of tears in her dark brown eyes. Her eyes closed as his finger trailed across her cheek.

'Everything will be OK.'

Unable to help himself, he kneeled before her and drew her into his arms, giving what comfort and support he could. Her arms slid round him, accepting, welcoming, and he closed his eyes, selfishly enjoying the feeling of her against him.

He knew she felt trapped, driven by her anxiety for her grandfather's safety to believe the only way out was to sacrifice herself. There was no way he was going to let her do it.

He sensed her withdrawal as she took a hold of her emotions, and he made himself move away. He returned to his chair and stared broodingly into the fire. A silence began to build between them, tense and awkward.

When Lexie rose to her feet and murmured something about preparing supper, Steve let her go, needing a few moments alone to think.

The dividing line between his feelings for Lexie and the job he was supposed to be doing was becoming murky. He had gone way past being professional. Now his feelings were far more personal.

10

'So what happens to your father's personal fortune when the deadline passes and you haven't married Costa?'

Lexie smiled at Steve's certainty. They were sitting at the table and taking a leisurely time over the appetising stew she had heated through for supper.

Since telling Steve about what had been going on, she felt slightly more in control. Clearly her concern for her grandfather and her lack of sleep had contributed to her display of emotion that afternoon — and to the way she had clung to Steve like a limpet to a rock.

Only it hadn't been comfort alone she had felt in his arms, Lexie admitted to herself. There had been heightened awareness, a tingle of excitement mixed with her concern and her painful admissions.

Lexie cleared her throat, fighting an embarrassed blush at the direction of her thoughts. She reached out to help herself to a crusty brown roll and tried to concentrate on the question Steve had asked her. He looked at her now and his curiosity was disturbing.

'You have to realise that my father had no intentions of dying before he was ready. In his mind, there was no hurry to marry me off. Costa would benefit, learning and preparing himself to take the helm of the empire without the distractions of a wife, as my father was quoted as saying,' she added with a faint smile. 'His death was unexpected and no doubt the clause was a safeguard he never anticipated would be necessary. Even so, he wanted to make certain he had the final say over my life and that of the family.'

Lexie took a sip of water and continued with the story.

'Besides, I have a small trust fund that is due to mature soon. It was something my mother did for me and the only thing my father was unable to touch. He was determined I would be bound and delivered to Costa before I had any financial independence. For once in his life things didn't work out his way. If I don't marry Costa — '

'You won't,' Steve interrupted harshly, his tone surprising her as much as his intense gaze.

For several seconds as they looked at each other, she wondered at his leashed anger, the reasons why he had been withdrawn and preoccupied since her earlier revelations. Now she felt a shiver of inner recognition but drew in a steadying breath, determined to resist her attraction to him.

'The will decrees that in the event of his demands not being fulfilled, his extensive art collection and all his private funds go to his favourite gallery to create the Dimitri Olympios Memorial Wing.' A ripple of genuine laughter escaped her. 'My father never did an altruistic deed in his life. Even this, his parting shot to spite us all for our disobedience, is something to glorify himself.'

'Unbelievable,' Steve muttered and she nodded.

While they ate, she told him how she had planned and saved, preparing for the day she would make her escape and put her father's world behind her. It had been hard to leave her friends, but she had found sanctuary in this remote, Scottish glen.

He looked up and captured her gaze, his grey eyes dark with apology.

'Until I waltzed in and led them to you.'

'I'm glad it was you,' she confided, embarrassed the moment the words left her mouth.

He looked at her, the grey eyes warm.

'I mean, someone else may not have helped me. They would have just told Yannis where I was and left it at that.'

She wanted to ask him why he hadn't done just that. The question hovered on the tip of her tongue and then she thought better of it. Things were complicated enough without her revealing more than was wise. As far as Steve was concerned, he was doing a job. She knew that. Far better it was left that way.

'None of my family can understand that neither my father's money nor his possessions mean anything to me,' she said now to cover her confusion. 'I have always seen myself as British and have never been in tune with my Greek half. Don't get me wrong. I love Greece, the country and the people, but I couldn't live there — not as 'living' would be with Costa, anyway.'

Their supper finished, Lexie cleared away the plates and made some coffee while Steve attended to the fire. The evenings were still cool and the flames brought a warm glow and a comfort to the small room.

After handing Steve his mug, Lexie leaned back in her chair feeling more relaxed than she had in hours. She watched him from beneath her lashes, the subdued lights and the flickering flames casting shadows and angles to his handsome face.

'I guess you come from an incredibly normal family.'

Her words permeated his disturbing thoughts and he raised his gaze to hers, saw the warmth, the invitation to talk. It was not one he often accepted, but he wanted to now, here, with Lexie.

'Pretty much,' he allowed, aware just how different he and Lexie were. 'My parents are good people, good parents. We never had much of anything in the material sense, but Mum and Dad worked away in ordinary jobs to keep our home life ticking over. It was all very average — nothing spectacular.'

He watched Lexie to see what she would make of the picture he had described, but not a flicker crossed her expression, only interest and encouragement.

'Believe me, Steve, being wealthy is not all it's cracked up to be.

What you had, the love and caring, was far more valuable than material things. You can't buy love or health or happiness.' She smiled and curled up in the chair. 'You said you were in the army, is that what you'd always wanted?'

'Far from it,' he said now, a playful smile pulling his mouth. 'I was going to score the winning goal for England in the World Cup Finals, and that was after I'd scored a hat-trick for Manchester United in the FA Cup at Wembley!'

'So what happened to this football legend?' she teased.

'Sadly my passion was greater than my talent. I foundered by the wayside like so many other dreamers.'

'Why the army?'

'It seemed a viable and stable alternative to an uncertain job market and a demoralising life on the dole.'

'Is that experience talking?'

'In a way. I watched my sister marry young in search of financial security at the cost of her happiness,' he explained, leaning forwards and resting his arms on his knees. 'And I watched my brother lose his spirit as he tried for job after job without having any success. But that's enough about me,' he said finally, not used to talking about his life or his family. 'What about you? What plans did you have?'

'I don't think I allowed myself to think that far ahead. It was enough of a struggle trying to stay one step ahead of my father and his plans for me.'

'And when this is over?' he asked, shifting his gaze to the flames lest he failed to hide his longing. 'What will you do then?'

She shrugged, as if it was too soon to allow herself the possibility of a satisfactory outcome.

'Something with people, I guess. And I want a home, children, all the old-fashioned stuff.' She smiled.

They talked for hours, drinking coffee and divulging information they'd never

154

really shared with anyone before. Steve watched Lexie visibly relaxing and he was glad.

He wanted her to be able to trust him, to talk to him as a friend. There were so many things he wanted as far as Lexie was concerned and he realised he was prepared to wait for as long as it took. Lexie was incredibly important to him already but after everything she'd been through, he didn't want to crowd her by coming on too strong.

'I didn't realise how late it was,' Steve commented eventually, checking his watch. 'You should sleep, and tomorrow we'll talk to Mike and make some plans.'

She shifted self-consciously, battling her disappointment that the evening, the closeness between them, was over. Smothering a sigh, she walked with him to the front door.

'Have you everything you need in the cottage? No-one has been there for a while.'

'It's fine. I had the windows open

earlier, and I set a fire.'

They stood on the step, breathing in the chill night air, clean and fresh off the hills. Lexie glanced up at the blackness of the sky, picking out the few stars she knew.

'Until I came here, I never paid attention to the stars before,' she told him. 'In London, there are too many distracting lights to see them properly.'

She turned her head to look at him and found him watching her and not the sky, his face shadowed in the dim light of the porch. Her heart began to pound in her chest.

The breeze eddied and blew her untamed curls around her face, and she raised a hand to restrain them.

'Lexie . . . '

Her name was a husky whisper and she barely heard it for the drumming of her pulse in her ears. He was going to kiss her. She wanted it, yet was frightened it would destroy the control she was frantically trying to exert over her feelings for him. Even as she thought it, she knew the battle was already lost.

The first dart of pleasure as his lips brushed across hers, drove every thought and argument from her mind. A faint sigh escaped him, then he deepened the kiss, drawing her to him.

Lexie's arms slid round him of their own volition and she felt herself simply melt into him.

She uttered an involuntary complaint when he ended it. For several moments he just held her, his own breath ragged against her face, then his lids slowly lifted to reveal sooty-grey eyes dark with lingering passion. Slowly, he released her and stepped back.

'Good-night, Lexie.'

' 'Night.'

She couldn't bear to watch him walk away, so she moved inside and closed the door. As she forced herself to lock up and see to the fire, she felt she was walking on a cushion of air.

She lay sleepless in bed for hours, rolling this way and that. No matter how much she tried to concentrate her thoughts on her missing grandfather and the machinations of her family, it was Steve who invaded her consciousness and her dreams.

* * *

Steve swung the axe at the log on the block with a satisfying thwack. He hadn't slept a wink last night and had risen hoping some physical exertion would take his mind off the events of last night. But he knew it wasn't working.

It didn't matter how much he told himself that whatever kind of life she was living now, they came from different worlds.

He felt an overpowering tenderness for her, along with excitement, protectiveness, and a frightening feeling that he could spend the rest of his life with her.

He had joked with his mother for years that he would know when the time and the woman were right. He thought of Lexie and, deep in his soul, he knew that time was now. It was silly, selfish and completely idiotic. But the idea had come to him in the middle of the night, and he couldn't stop thinking about it.

Lexie stood in the kitchen waiting for the kettle to boil, and watched Steve chopping logs in the back garden. She felt mesmerised, hardly able to take her eyes off him . . . Pulling herself together, she opened the back door.

'Breakfast's nearly ready.'

A brisk wave was the only response, and she turned away, putting some bacon under the grill and scrambling some eggs. She had to stop thinking about him all the time.

There were more important things, namely her grandfather's safety, that should be occupying all her energies. But the memory of his kiss, the way she felt when she was with him . . .

'Madness,' she muttered to herself.

'Excuse me?'

Startled, Lexie swung round nearly upsetting the eggs, and looked at Steve, framed in the doorway.

'What?'

'I thought you said something.'

'No,' she fibbed. 'It was nothing.'

When they sat down to breakfast, she realised they were both still wary after the kiss they had shared. Steve appeared preoccupied, lost in thought, and her own emotions were too raw and confused to share.

After a while, his plate cleaned, he sat back on the chair and watched her. Lexie shifted nervously under that assessing gaze.

'What is it?' she asked at last, unable to maintain her cool.

An enigmatic smile curbed his sensuous mouth.

'Lexie, will you marry me?'

11

Everything had happened so quickly. Lexie hovered in the doorway of the London registry office, still in a daze after the last frantic days. How on earth had Steve managed to persuade her to go along with this insane scheme?

She had said it was crazy right from the moment she had recovered her wits following his surprise question. Apart from anything else, her emotions were too involved with him to view the suggestion in a dispassionate light:

'Think about it,' Steve had persisted, despite all her protests. 'If you are already married to someone else, your father's conditions cannot be met. There is absolutely nothing your family can do,' he emphasised.

Lexie looked at the black, rain-filled sky and wrapped her coat more tightly around her against the chill air. She should never have let Steve talk her round, however much he had insisted that the ploy would work. Clearly he had thought it all out, even down to the quiet annulment once the deadline had passed.

'It's just a means to an end, Lexie. Then it will be over and you'll be free.'

It had been impossible to explain to herself why his assurances had made her feel even worse. He had been so businesslike about the whole thing, as if it was just part of the job he had promised to do.

But here she was, Mrs Westwood, albeit in name only. She couldn't believe how easy it had been to get married. Within one working day after filling out the forms and applying for the special licence, you could become a legal couple. There was something rather sad about it.

There had been so much activity in the last few days she had barely had time to think. After reluctantly agreeing to Steve's plan of action, there had been so much to do, from arranging time off work to the formalities here in London.

In between had come the confirmation from Mike that they had a lead on her grandfather through Yannis. Then there had been the thrilling motorbike ride south, when she had clung to Steve, the wind whipping her hair free of its restraint under the helmet. It had been exhilarating, but that feeling had rapidly subsided the closer they came to their destination.

Tomorrow she would see her grandfather, know he was safe, and have the satisfaction of thwarting her family. Steve had made that possible, along with Mike's help. But at what cost to her feelings for Steve? She didn't dare examine that side of things.

'Lexie!'

The sound of her name drew her from her confused and unhappy thoughts. Sheltering under her umbrella, she crossed the pavement to join Steve who stood with his partner Mike, and Mike's pretty blonde wife, Andrea, who had been their witnesses.

'Is everything set up for tomorrow?' Mike asked now.

'I spoke to Yannis and he promised to have my grandfather in his office at nine. He knows nothing,' Lexie added, recalling her cousin's victorious smugness as she had delivered her carefully rehearsed speech.

'OK.' Mike turned from her to Steve. 'I'll meet you as arranged.'

Steve nodded and hailed a cruising taxi for Mike and Andrea who had to dash off and pick up their children from an after-school birthday party.

'Thanks for your help.'

'No problem. Nice to meet you, Lexie.' Andrea smiled.

'You, too,' she replied as Mike's wife slid into the car.

'We'll see you both later,' Steve said as Mike got into the taxi beside her.

Once the taxi had eased into the stream of rush-hour traffic, Steve linked his arm in Lexie's, sharing the umbrella, and they walked in silence along the street. It wasn't far to his rented flat that had been home for the last couple of days, but she was glad of the delay at being there alone with him.

She was quiet, withdrawn, her thoughts a jumble of emotions — pleasure at knowing she would soon see her grandfather; anxiety at facing Yannis and the family wrath; growing distress at the situation she found herself in with Steve and her feelings for him.

The memory of their one kiss and the emotions it had roused within her still lingered. But it was so much more than basic, physical attraction with him. She admired him, respected him, cared about him for the person he was. They had been thrown together in unusual circumstances, and consequently, she had come to know him in a short time.

And however much she told herself her feelings couldn't be trusted while she had other pressures to contend with, that Steve's part in securing her grandfather's safety played a part in her feelings, she knew that they grew stronger and more involved with each passing hour.

She smothered a sigh, aware of him beside her. Her feelings weren't going to disappear with the ending of the family threat. And the involvement of her heart, her burgeoning love for Steve, could not be annulled as easily as a paper marriage.

Steve knew something was wrong. Lexie had been growing quieter and quieter, and a troubled frown pulled her brow. Suddenly, he couldn't face hours alone with her in his flat knowing the wedding they had just undertaken was a sham . . . and all the time wishing it wasn't.

Mike had questioned his motives when he had explained his foolproof plan. What a joke that was. He was being a prize fool over Lexie. But he had shrugged off his friend's concerns with a show of bravado, unwilling to admit just how much Lexie had come to mean to him.

'How about we have an early dinner?' he suggested, unwilling to travel the dangerous route of his thoughts.

Lexie looked up at him, her eyes darker than ever in her drawn face.

'OK.'

'What's wrong?' he asked, detecting the listlessness in her voice that was usually so vibrant and thrilling to his senses.

'I was just thinking about tomorrow,' she replied, lowering her gaze.

Steve didn't believe her but he decided not to press the point. They were both tired after the rush of the last few days, and she felt tense next to him. The growing tension bothered him. This had been a really silly idea.

They both seemed to make an effort to relax and act normally as they chatted over dinner. She was so easy to talk to, smart and funny, and he loved being with her. They argued over sport and films, discussed books and environmental issues, laughed at childhood pranks.

As if neither of them wanted the spell to end, they lingered over their sweets and coffee. Soon they could not put off the inevitable any longer, and once they left the restaurant, he was disappointed that Lexie seemed to retreat into herself once more.

Back at his flat, she murmured an excuse and went to have a bath. For a while he watched television but none of the programmes held his interest.

When at last Lexie re-emerged, flushed from the hot water, her glorious black curls damp at the ends, his heart kicked uncomfortably in his chest.

'If you don't mind, I think I'll have an early night,' she said, immediately deflating his thoughts of spending more time with her. 'It's been a long day and I want to be fresh for tomorrow.'

Steve curbed his selfish disappointment and rose to his feet. He moved towards her, resisting the overwhelming temptation to take her in his arms and tell her how he was feeling about her. But she had enough to cope with for now. Instead, he tried to lighten the tension between them, wanted to see her smile again.

'Don't I at least get a kiss, then?' he teased with a playful smile. 'It is our wedding night after all.'

He was horrified when Lexie began to cry. What had he said? He wanted to hold her, comfort her, but when he stepped closer and reached out to her, she looked up at him with wounded eyes and backed away.

'I'm sorry,' he managed, his voice rough with confusion and dismay. 'I was just teasing.'

She wiped impatiently at tears on her cheeks, and edged towards the doorway of the spare bedroom.

'No, I'm sorry. Good-night,' she whispered.

He stared at the closed door for countless minutes, fighting the numbing disappointment, the confusion, the bitter realisation that Lexie was not in the least interested in him. He had offered her a way out of her problem and she had reluctantly accepted. There was nothing personal. How could he be so idiotic?

Lexie lay in bed unable to sleep, mortified at her emotional display. Steve had looked unnerved and upset at her reaction to his innocent teasing, and she couldn't blame him. He must think he was harbouring a mad woman.

She rolled over on to her stomach and slid an arm beneath the springy pillow. The stress of the day had been too much, she allowed. She had been on edge, trying to keep her emotions in check and her feelings for him hidden, all the time wishing that he cared, that it was real.

Finally she slept, a restless, broken sleep, that saw her waking feeling lethargic and unsettled. She washed and dressed with care for her meeting with Yannis. The nerves had started already. Smelling freshly-made coffee, she took a deep breath and went in search of Steve.

The kitchen was empty, so she helped herself to a cup and wandered towards the archway to the living-room. She hesitated when she saw him. Dressed in a similar charcoal suit to the one he had worn to the registry office the day before, he was leaning against the windowsill, his forehead resting on the cool glass of the pane.

Even in profile he looked troubled and unhappy. She felt an upsurge of guilt, both at what he had done for her with little gratitude on her part, and for her behaviour the night before.

'Morning.'

She licked her lips that had turned suddenly dry when he turned to face her, the grey eyes watchful and enigmatic. 'Steve, about last night — '

'It doesn't matter. It was thoughtless of me.'

Her gaze slid towards the carpet to hide her dismay.

'Of course, if that's what you want.'

'Can I get you some breakfast?'

'No, thank you. Coffee is fine.'

She hated this stilted politeness between them. He seemed so unapproachable, and the easy closeness they had shared before the marriage the day before had gone.

Steve glanced at his watch, a frown on his face.

'Well, if you're ready, I suggest we go and get this over with.'

'That's fine with me,' Lexie responded briskly, spinning on her heel and grabbing her coat and handbag.

Whatever it took, she would somehow get through the day. But she just couldn't imagine how she would be able to walk away from Steve and ever be whole again.

Steve stared morosely out of the taxi window. The rain had stopped, but the sky was still leaden with no hint of the spring sun that had warmed the glen a few days before.

Mike was waiting for them as arranged and at exactly nine o'clock, the three of them walked purposefully through the plush reception area of the solicitor's suite of offices. The same unappealing secretary he had encountered on his first visit rose uncertainly from behind the desk but Steve ignored her.

The ornate doors to the Greek's office stood ajar, and with a hand on Lexie's back, he guided her forward. His gaze swept the oversize room. Yannis Apostolakis sat behind his desk looking smug and puffed up with his own importance. Nearby sat a grey-haired man with a neat beard whom Steve identified as Lexie's grandfather. He looked anxious but in good shape.

The third occupant of the room was unknown to him. Young, but already running to seed from overindulgence, he stepped out of the shadows of an alcove and swaggered arrogantly towards them. He heard Lexie's indrawn breath, felt her stiffen and instinctively move closer to his side, and he sensed a flicker of fear.

'Costa!' She spoke his name almost as an exclamation.

Steve's gaze narrowed as he assessed the younger man, and he noted with anger and a sense of possession he had no right to feel, the salacious way his eyes watched Lexie. His hand increased its pressure on her back and he steered her away from Costa and towards her grandfather who had risen from his chair at their arrival.

'Gramps!'

Lexie moved away from Steve and rushed to meet her grandfather who enveloped her in a hug.

'I'm fine, Lexie, don't worry.'

Steve met Yannis Apostolakis's cold gaze.

'So, Mr Westwood, it seems you found our Miss Bennett after all.'

Conscious that Mike was keeping a watchful eye behind him, Steve deliberately placed himself between Lexie and Costa. He glanced briefly at Alisdair Bennett.

'Excuse me, sir. Would you join

Mike by the door, please.'

Without waiting to see that his request was met, but sensing compliance, Steve focused his gaze on Yannis once more.

'No, Mr Apostolakis,' he answered now in measured tones. 'You see, she isn't Ms Bennett any more. She isn't even Miss Olympios.'

Watching the changing expression on Yannis's face, Steve slipped his arm proprietarily round Lexie's waist and drew her unresistingly towards him.

'In future, you will address her as Mrs Westwood. Lexie is now my wife.'

12

Alexandra, I forbid this!' Yannis roared, slamming his fists on the desk as he rose to his feet, his face contorted with anger.

'You have no say in what I decide to do with my life,' Lexie responded with quiet strength, gaining courage from Steve's presence, the feel of his arm around her. She leaned into him. 'Our marriage is legal and above board, and we have a copy of the certificate here to prove it.'

Yannis thrust aside the paper she handed him.

'This is outrageous.'

'There's nothing outrageous about falling in love,' Steve intervened with calm amusement.

'Love?' Costa spat, his expression murderous. 'She has nothing without me. You won't see a penny of the money. Alexandra is mine.'

She felt Steve's anger in the way he went still, his body rigid against her. Glancing up, she saw his eyes were narrowed, battleship grey, immovable and dangerous as he faced Costa.

'Lexie is her own person, not a possession. I have no interest in money, only in spending the rest of my life with her.'

The words cut to her heart, and for several moments, she forgot to breathe. But she knew it wasn't true. Steve was putting on a great performance as the loving, protective husband, but that was all it was. A performance. An act.

Disappointment and sadness welled within her. Between one heartbeat and the next, she realised just how much she had come to love this man. Loved him, but had to walk away.

'Don't try to come near Lexie or her grandfather again.' Steve warned with underlying menace as he began to guide her towards the door. 'This stops now or we take it to the authorities.'

As they left the office, Mike and Lexie's grandfather a few paces ahead of them, she could hear Costa and Yannis arguing violently in Greek. A shiver ran through her and Steve tightened his hold.

'What do you think they'll do?' she asked softly as they crossed the reception area.

'They'll huff and they'll puff for a while, but there isn't anything they can do, Lexie.'

She hesitated and Steve came to a halt and looked down at her, concern and enquiry in his eyes.

'Thank you,' she whispered. 'Thank you for doing this.'

The grey eyes warmed and darkened, his free hand rising to brush some stray curls back from her face.

'No problem. Come on,' he added, tugging her arm. 'Let's go and see your grandfather.'

Lexie drew in a breath, trying to capture in her memory the way he had looked at her, the way it had sent a prickle of heated awareness all over her body.

When they stepped out on to the pavement, Mike had already hailed a passing taxi and held the door open for them. Reluctantly, Lexie moved out of Steve's hold and joined her grandfather inside.

'Are you all right?' she asked, turning an anxious gaze to him as he started to cough.

His hazel eyes twinkled with amusement.

'Can't say I'd want to do it every day, but I'm not so old I can't have a wee adventure now and then.'

He chuckled, taking his plight with equanimity.

Lexie couldn't help but laugh. It was so wonderful to have him back with her safe and sound, and the old rogue actually seemed to be enjoying himself. All her relief at seeing him, at having the shadow of Costa removed from her, and her love for her grandfather shone through as she hugged him.

'There now, girlie, don't go soft on me!'

He drew back with a smile and glanced at Steve as he stepped into the taxi and sat down.

'Mike and I have been introduced, but I understand this is the man I have to thank.'

Lexie nodded and glanced at Steve from under her lashes.

'Yes. Gramps, this is Steve Westwood.'

'You certainly know how to make an entrance.' Her grandfather laughed, pumping his hand. 'I appreciate you taking care of Lexie.'

She felt the touch of Steve's gaze as he answered.

'It was my pleasure.'

As the taxi wended its way back towards Steve's flat, Lexie leaned back and watched as Steve and her grandfather chatted away like old friends. She was ridiculously pleased that they had struck up an instant rapport.

A faint movement from Mike, who sat on the fold-down seat across from her, drew her attention. With a jolt, she realised he had been watching her watching Steve, that the alert interest in his eyes, the dawning smile on his mouth, meant he had some insight into her feelings. She froze, horrified, then dragged her gaze away to stare sightlessly from the window. Would Mike give her away?

'I'll go into the office for a while to give you two some quiet time alone,' Steve announced as the taxi drew to a halt.

Lexie nodded, avoiding both Steve's and Mike's gazes as she stepped out to join her grandfather on the pavement. She hovered uncertainly for a moment.

'We'll see you later then,' she mumbled awkwardly, then closed the door.

Two hours later, Steve regretted his decision to come to the office. His inefficient ways had offended Joyce, and he had taken some ribbing from

Mike with ill grace. It was all Lexie's fault.

He sat moodily at his desk and sifted through his paperwork. The files seemed to have multiplied at an alarming rate in the few days he had been away but his heart wasn't in the job of catching up on his other cases. And that was all this was, albeit somewhat unusual, he lectured himself. A case. Except he knew it wasn't.

He had known from the first it was a mistake to get involved with her, but he had gone right ahead and done it anyway. And now he didn't know what to do. He was within a whisker of losing her. Any time now she would head back to Scotland with her grandfather and in a few months their *paper marriage* could be annulled. The thought depressed him.

With a sigh, he closed the file in front of him and leaned back in his chair. How could he keep his mind on anything when all he could think about was Lexie.

'You're in love with her, aren't you?'

Mike's question interrupted his thoughts, and he focused a wary gaze on his friend.

'Yeah,' he admitted at last, tired of lying about his feelings.

'What are you going to do about it?'

'I don't know.'

'That's not like you to give up so easily.'

'If she was interested, maybe I wouldn't have to.'

'You're just going to let her walk away?'

'What else can I do?'

'Go on, get out of here,' Mike urged. 'You need to talk to her and get it sorted out. Oh,' he added with a smug smile, 'a word of advice.'

'What?'

'Take off that blindfold you're wearing.'

He was puzzled by Mike's cryptic remark, but he needed no second invitation to go to see Lexie. At least he was doing something positive and not moping about it. Feeling better, he even gave Joyce a broad smile as he passed the reception desk . . .

'You really care for this man, don't you, Lexie?'

'Yes, yes I do.' She knew better than to deny anything with Gramps. He was far too astute. 'But Steve is just doing a job. There isn't anything between us.'

'I wouldn't be too sure about that,' he advised, a knowing sparkle in his hazel eyes. 'Now, I have a few old friends to look up to share a dram or two. You have a chat with this man of yours when he gets back.'

Lexie smiled in return, but left alone in Steve's flat, she was tormented by indecision and confusion. She had a couple of things she wanted to do before she left London, see Jillian and a few other friends, pay a visit to Mrs Peterson. But she couldn't impose on Steve's hospitality.

He had been kind and patient, but she couldn't expect him to cater to her

184

and her grandfather now the family business was over.

Only all this wasn't quite over, she allowed, wandering into the spare room. There was still the question of waiting for the deadline on her father's will to pass and then her marriage to Steve could be annulled. He would be free. She doubted she would ever be free of her longing for him.

Sadly, she began to gather her belongings together. It would be best if she went today. The longer it dragged on, the harder it would be to make herself leave him behind in London and return to Scotland. She hadn't thought she could ever live in the city again, but the peaceful beauty of the glen did not have the same appeal as it had a few days ago. Wherever Steve was, she wanted to be there, too.

'Lexie?'

She spun round at the sound of his voice. He was leaning in the doorway, his tie askew, his hair rumpled, his gaze wary. Her hand lifted to cover the rapid pulse at her throat.

'You startled me.'

He glanced past her to the back pack lying on the bed.

'You're leaving?'

'I'm sure you'll be glad to see the back of me,' she attempted to joke, but her effort at humour fell flat. 'I've caused enough disruption in your life and taken up enough of your agency's time.'

Unable to face him, daunted by his set expression and his stormy grey eyes, she turned away and began stuffing things haphazardly into her bag.

'In a few months, you'll be able to get an annulment,' she continued, cursing the waver in her voice. 'I know this has just been a job to you, and — '

'What are you talking about, Lexie?' he cursed, pushing himself away from the door and crossing the room. 'Is that all I've been to you in this, some kind of hired help?'

Dismayed at his anger, she looked

right through him, unable to look him in the eye.

'I didn't mean that. I can never thank you enough for what you have done for me, and I'll never forget . . . ' she amended hastily.

She could hardly bear to say goodbye. She felt bound to this man and knew a closeness that went way beyond the reason they had been together. She had never known love could be so painful. Blindly, she reached for a jumper that lay on the bed, but Steve snatched it out of her hand.

'Lexie, stop. I can't do this.'

A heavy weight settled in the pit of her stomach as her gaze clashed with his.

'You mean you want an annulment now?' she questioned, somehow managing to force out the words.

'No.' He dragged his fingers through the springy thickness of his hair. 'No, that's not it at all.'

'If Yannis and Costa find out the marriage isn't real — '

'They won't.'

He walked away from her and stared out of the window for a moment before he murmured something she didn't hear.

'I'm sorry?'

He spun to face her.

'I said, we could always make it real.'

For a few dizzying seconds, Lexie was convinced the world had stopped turning. Were her ears playing some cruel trick on her? Was this a joke?

'Are you serious?'

'I don't want you to go.' He drew in a breath. 'Everything I said in that office this morning was the truth. The first time I saw you, I knew.' Again he seemed to falter for a second, his gaze uncertain, as if he hardly dared to trust her to hear what he had to say, then huskily, he went on, 'I love you, Lexie.'

Tears of happiness and disbelief stung her eyes. She hardly dared believe it was true, and yet she could tell what it had cost him to say the words to her.

'So there you go.' He blew out a shaky breath and turned away from her again. 'I've never said that to anyone before.'

Lexie thought her heart would burst as she crossed the room and stepped between him and the window.

'Steve . . . ' She breathed his name and reached up a hand to his cheek.

'Have I made an idiot of myself?'

'No more than me. The thing is, I love you, too.'

She laughed at the change of expression on his face as anxiety faded to disbelief and was soon replaced by happiness and a warming passion. He pulled her to him and kissed her with the kind of pent-up emotion she understood only too well because she shared it.

'I've always fancied living in a place like your glen,' Steve confided, pulling away from her. 'I was thinking perhaps we could persuade the landowner to sell us the cottages. We could go there for long week-ends and holidays, and have the best of both worlds. What do you think, Mrs Westwood?'

He eased her head back a fraction so he could look at her while he waited for her answer. Lexie smiled up at him, her dark eyes lit with a vivacious shine.

'I think, Mr Westwood, that you can read my mind.'

'If the business keeps growing, maybe I can even persuade Mike that we should open a Scottish office.'

Lexie laughed and reached up a hand to draw his mouth back to hers, excitement coursing through her at the thought of a lifetime with Steve.

He hesitated a moment, teasing her, his lips a hairbreadth from hers.

'Where's your grandfather?'

'Out visiting old friends,' she responded, a touch breathless.

'Good.'

His eyes turned warm and smoky with the kind of look that made her toes curl. As she met and matched the wonder of his kiss, she marvelled at her fortune — a fortune greater than the monetary one her father had amassed, a fortune that could never be measured anywhere but the heart.

Steve had helped her banish the legacy of her father's dominance and sever the bonds of her unhappy past. Now, together, they could look forward to an exciting, loving future making family ties of their own.

THE END

Other titles in the Linford Romance Library

SAVAGE PARADISE
Sheila Belshaw

For four years, Diana Hamilton had dreamed of returning to Luangwa Valley in Zambia. Now she was back — and, after a close encounter with a rhino — was receiving a lecture from a tall, khaki-clad man on the dangers of going into the bush alone!

PAST BETRAYALS
Giulia Gray

As soon as Jon realized that Julia had fallen in love with him, he broke off their relationship and returned to work in the Middle East. When Jon's best friend, Danny, proposed a marriage of friendship, Julia accepted. Then Jon returned and Julia discovered her love for him remained unchanged.

PRETTY MAIDS ALL IN A ROW
Rose Meadows

The six beautiful daughters of George III of England dreamt of handsome princes coming to claim them, but the King always found some excuse to reject proposals of marriage. This is the story of what befell the Princesses as they began to seek lovers at their father's court, leaving behind rumours of secret marriages and illegitimate children.

THE GOLDEN GIRL
Paula Lindsay

Sarah had everything — wealth, social background, great beauty and magnetic charm. Her heart was ruled by love and compassion for the less fortunate in life. Yet, when one man's happiness was at stake, she failed him — and herself.

A DREAM OF HER OWN
Barbara Best
A stranger gently kisses Sarah Danbury at her Betrothal Ball. Little does she realise that she is to meet this mysterious man again in very different circumstances.

HOSTAGE OF LOVE
Nara Lake
From the moment pretty Emma Tregear, the only child of a Van Diemen's Land magnate, met Philip Despard, she was desperately in love. Unfortunately, handsome Philip was a convict on parole.

THE ROAD TO BENDOUR
Joyce Eaglestone
Mary Mackenzie had lived a sheltered life on the family farm in Scotland. When she took a job in the city she was soon in a romantic maze from which only she could find the way out.

NEW BEGINNINGS
Ann Jennings
On the plane to his new job in a hospital in Turkey, Felix asked Harriet to put their engagement on hold, as Philippe Krir, the Director of Bodrum hospital, refused to hire 'attached' people. But, without an engagement ring, what possible excuse did Harriet have for holding Philippe at bay?

THE CAPTAIN'S LADY
Rachelle Edwards
1820: When Lianne Vernon becomes governess at Elswick Manor, she finds her young pupil is given to strange imaginings and that her employer, Captain Gideon Lang, is the most enigmatic man she has ever encountered. Soon Lianne begins to fear for her pupil's safety.

THE VAUGHAN PRIDE
Margaret Miles

As the new owner of Southwood Manor, Laura Vaughan discovers that she's even more poverty stricken than before. She also finds that her neighbour, the handsome Marius Kerr, is a little too close for comfort.

HONEY-POT
Mira Stables

Lovely, well-born, well-dowered, Russet Ingram drew all men to her. Yet here she was, a prisoner of the one man immune to her graces — accused of frivolously tampering with his young ward's romance!

DREAM OF LOVE
Helen McCabe

When there is a break-in at the art gallery she runs, Jade can't believe that Corin Bossinney is a trickster, or that she'd fallen for the oldest trick in the book . . .

FOR LOVE OF OLIVER
Diney Delancey

When Oliver Scott buys her family home, Carly retains the stable block from which she runs her riding school. But she soon discovers Oliver is not an easy neighbour to have. Then Carly is presented with a new challenge, one she must face for love of Oliver.

THE SECRET OF MONKS' HOUSE
Rachelle Edwards

Soon after her arrival at Monks' House, Lilith had been told that it was haunted by a monk, and she had laughed. Of greater interest was their neighbour, the mysterious Fabian Delamaye. Was he truly as debauched as rumour told, and what was the truth about his wife's death?

THE SPANISH HOUSE
Nancy John

Lynn couldn't help falling in love with the arrogant Brett Sackville. But Brett refused to believe that she felt nothing for his half-brother, Rafael. Lynn knew that the cruel game Brett made her play to protect Rafael's heart could end only by breaking hers.

PROUD SURGEON
Lynne Collins

Calder Savage, the new Senior Surgical Officer at St. Antony's Hospital, had really lived up to his name, venting a savage irony on anyone who fell foul of him. But when he gave Staff Nurse Honor Portland a lift home, she was surprised to find what an interesting man he was.

A PARTNER FOR PENNY
Pamela Forest

Penny had grown up with Christopher Lloyd and saw in him the older brother she'd never had. She was dismayed when he was arrogantly confident that she should not trust her new business colleague, Gerald Hart. She opposed Chris by setting out to win Gerald as a partner both in love and business.

SURGEON ASHORE
Ann Jennings

Luke Roderick, the new Consultant Surgeon for Accident and Emergency, couldn't understand why Staff Nurse Naomi Selbourne refused to apply for the vacant post of Sister. Naomi wasn't about to tell him that she moonlighted as a waitress in order to support her small nephew, Toby.

A MOONLIGHT MEETING
Peggy Gaddis

Megan seemed to have fallen under handsome Tom Fallon's spell, and she was no longer sure if she would be happy as Larry's wife. It was only in the aftermath of a terrible tragedy that she realized the true meaning of love.

THE STARLIT GARDEN
Patricia Hemstock

When interior designer Tansy Donaghue accepted a commission to restore Beechwood Manor in Devon, she was relieved to leave London and its memories of her broken romance with architect Robert Jarvis. But her dream of a peaceful break was shattered not only by Robert's unexpected visit, but also by the manipulative charms of the manor's owner, James Buchanan.